# No Mortals Allowed

**What If Myth, Volume 1**

Honey Beezleigh

Published by Honey Beezleigh, 2021.

# Also by Honey Beezleigh

**What If Myth**
No Mortals Allowed
The Two Lives of Ariadne
The Wrong Princess

Watch for more at https://honeybeezleigh.com/.

# Table of Contents

# Chapter 1

ARIADNE SAT ON A ROCK at the edge of the encampment, surveying the busy followers of the god of wine. The majority of them were his female followers, the maenads, but there were more than a few of the distinctly male satyrs. The general lack of clothing was a hallmark of the following of Dionysus, where the festivals famously tended to descend into drunken orgies.

They all wore the symbols of their god, crowned in vines or carrying large staffs topped with pine cones. Several wore the draped spotted furs of animals she had only heard about. A few wore only animal furs and nothing else. The air was fresh and crisp, with the promise of heady midday heat tempering its bite.

"Whatcha looking at?" A very pretty maenad leaned over Ariadne's shoulder, long black curls falling forward.

"The traveling camp of the wine god. It's a lot busier than I thought it would be." Ariadne brushed the other woman's silky hair from her face but more just fell in its place, leaving her view full of hair.

"The festival tonight is going to be amazing. But all the festivals are, really." The maenad seemed to be agreeing to something, and sat next to Ariadne with a flop of splayed limbs and bouncing hair. "I'm Nysa." She introduced herself casually.

Ariadne could feel her eyes widen at how far up the other woman's skirt had risen and swallowed, averting her gaze. "Ariadne." She offered her name in turn, not bothering with her royal title. She asked, "This festival is based around a ceremony to dedicate wine to the patron god Dionysus, right?" She asked, despite knowing the answer.

"Yep. Why, you got something you're going to dedicate?" Nysa's pale green eyes gleamed as she twisted her whole body to face Ariadne, skirt riding higher and revealing her bare thighs.

Ariadne chewed her lip, and tried not to look. "Maybe. I want to, but I really struggled making it and don't want to offend. It tastes like death." She admitted with a groan, throwing herself backwards, completely forgetting she was sitting on unforgiving stone and not grass.

Instead of Ariadne's head hitting hard rock strong hands buffered the impact. She opened her eyes to see the face of the concerned looking Nysa.

Instead of commenting on Ariadne's fumble or embarrassed flush, Nysa said, "I've been to quite a few of these shindigs. I could try your wine and tell you if it will be offensive."

Ariadne sat up and snatched the other woman's hands, checking them for damage. "Are you okay? What were you thinking?" She didn't see any bruises but they could still show up.

"I could say the same thing to you, throwing yourself back against a rock like that." Nysa countered, letting Ariadne prod and examine her hands.

They were smooth, with perfectly painted glassy green nails without blemish. On closer inspection they were not soft in all places, with rough callouses in areas. Realizing she was stroking the other woman's hand, Ariadne dropped Nysa's hands with a cough. "I'm glad you're not hurt."

Nysa grinned at her, "The wine would be good." She leaned in to brush Ariadne's hair behind her ear and traced the shell of it with the edge of her nail.

Ariadne sat there, stunned for a minute before she registered the words through her tingling ears. "Yes. The wine. You wanted to try it." Her tongue is awkward in her mouth. She reached into the bag beside her and pulled out the heavy jug of wine. "I don't have glasses." She realized.

"I do!" The maenad waves two wine glasses at her that Ariadne had no idea where she pulled them from. Benefits of being a follower of the god of wine, she supposed.

Ariadne poured a bare finger width of wine for the other woman. "Stingy!" Nysa mock gasped, holding a hand over her wide smile.

"This is awful wine. You need to know that. I'm not sure what I was thinking bringing it here." She added in a mutter to herself, despite knowing she hadn't cared about the taste of the wine. It was a chance to get out, if she could be accepted into the traveling followers of Dionysus.

"I'll be the judge of that." Nysa drank and immediately spat the wine back out, coughing and wheezing.

Ariadne sighed and dug in her bag for a cloth, handing it to the wine splattered woman. "I suppose that answers that question."

"Where did you make this?" She wheezed, mopping her face gently to not smear her makeup.

Ariadne let her gaze drift to the horizon where the walls of the labyrinth loomed over the city below it. "A graveyard. Like I said, I don't know what I was thinking." Mostly that the Minotaur hated green things and wouldn't eat grape vines. Even if it would have been better for the rest of the world if he had. Grapes were less precious than children, after all.

The other woman followed her gaze, eyes sharpening at the sight of the looming labyrinth. "I don't know, it was wine. Terrible wine, but still wine."

Ariadne snorted. "Would you put it in your mouth again?"

Nysa closed her mouth. "No." She admitted. "Still, Dionysus appreciates all efforts at making wine. Some people are just more talented than others. But, a graveyard, really?"

"It's all I had available for space." Ariadne defended, then added thoughtfully, "Do you think I should dedicate it to the Gods of the Underworld? Give them something to serve unwanted guests?" Hades had a reputation for discouraging even divine visitors to his realm with the exception of his Queen, Persephone.

Nysa grinned, face stretching into a terrible expression that reminded Ariadne that the sacrifices to the god of wine used to include human dismemberment. "He would like that." She answered far too knowingly for Ariadne's comfort.

"Will I still be welcome tonight, even though I don't have a sacrifice?" Ariadne glanced at the camp setting up and bit her lip.

"Don't worry about it. You tried. Besides, I can make you my plus one." Nysa gave Ariadne an appreciative once over, followed by her hands trailing down Ariadne's sides to clasp her hands. "If you'd like."

Ariadne returned the look and realized something about her companion. "Are you a man?"

Nysa raised a perfectly painted eyebrow. They challenged, "Does it matter?"

"No, but I don't have any," Ariadne's face was on fire and she pulled a hand free to gesture at her lower abdomen, tongue suddenly in knots. "For being with a man." Granted, the doctor had told her she was sterile when her period had failed to arrive, but a baby wasn't a surprise she wanted. Ever.

"Contraceptives." Ariadne blurted out, finally remembering the right word. She wanted a hole to open up in the ground to swallow her.

Nysa's expression softened. "I understand. I can get you some, no problem. But there are other things that can be fun that don't require any contraceptive measures if you'd like, instead." They wiggled their eyebrows at Ariadne, hands sliding back up her arms slowly.

"Both?" Ariadne wiggled her eyebrows back, hoping this was the correct confirmation signal, making her laugh.

"Both." Nysa agreed with a purr, pulling her in for a kiss.

ARIADNE woke up to the smell of flowers, heady enough to choke on. Light crept needle thin fingers of light through the tent flap gap, illuminating the room. Nysa lay face down on Ariadne's lap, the both of them naked. The leopard skin covering them both had slipped off and puddled on the floor.

Ariadne observed all this as she drifted awake, puzzle pieces about her new lover from the night before slotting into place. Drank like a fish and remained standing and flirting, check. Danced like a wild thing possessed, check. Unusual sexual stamina, check.

She could have passed all that off as traits of servants of the wine god or having not much previous experience with lovers without a second thought. She could have even passed off their eyes bleeding from pale green to glowing during sex as a trick of the light.

But the damn wine. It was always on hand, whether there had been a jug there before or not. After a certain point, there hadn't even been a jug, just never emptying cups of wine. Ariadne's head didn't even hurt from drinking what had to have been at least three bottles of wine.

"The wine gave you away." She told the god of wine in her lap lazily, carding fingers through his hair.

"Was wondering if you would say something about it." Dionysus mumbled into her bare thighs, rolling over with a sigh and blinking sleepily up at her through a tangle of hair.

"I wasn't sure if you were honestly trying for undercover or just trying to give hints without coming out and saying it." She traced his makeup smeared green eyes. God or not, they left them looking like a badly masked bandit.

"Bit of both." Dionysus yawned, stretching like a cat and then settling back in her lap to blink sleepily up at her. "Did you have fun?"

Ariadne grinned, feeling her whole body flush at the memories. "Definitely."

Dionysus leered up at her. "Want to do it again?"

She leered back down at them. "Definitely."

<hr>

"Did you honestly think you would get away with it?" The leader of King Minos's personal guard scoffed, kicking her in the ribs with a booted foot and sending her sprawling over her picked flowers.

Ariadne had honestly thought she had gotten away with it. It had been two full days since she had ran away from her upcoming 'duties' and no one had come after her. Stepping foot outside the camp grounds to pick flowers had been a mistake. But the wild roses had reminded her of how her new lover made her feel and she had sat down and woven a crown, careful of the sharp thorns.

She hunched over it, looking up through her eyelashes at the guard, stomach sinking as she counted four more guards with him. The soldiers all wore the markings of elite soldiers from the brutal war with Athens. The other country had conceded to tributes being sent to the Minotaur out of desperation to stem the tide of slaughter. Fourteen children every seven years was a terrible price, but cheaper than what they had been paying.

Ariadne looked toward the camp, colorful tents and banners fluttering in the warm wind. If she screamed, the camp would wake and come for her. They would come and the peaceful, friendly partiers would die. Her lover had went back up to Olympus that morning with a leer and promise to 'come again'.

She set the crown of wild roses down, fingers bloodying the white petals. "Fine. Let's go then." She lifted her chin at the head guard like the princess she was, and not the prisoner she felt like.

The guard backhanded her casually, sending her sprawling into the flowers again. "None of that, princess. You abandoned your post, so you don't get any of its privileges." He leaned down and grabbed her by the front her dress to give her an up close view of his ghastly amusement. "King Minos said tonight you're to go with the tributes inside the labyrinth. No room for traitors in the royal family."

He jerked her to her feet and hauled her over his shoulder like a sack of vegetables, grinding her flower crown under his heel. The soldiers didn't even look at the camp as they left, it was like they couldn't even see it. Ariadne tried to be grateful for the small mercies.

# Chapter 2

ATHENS SENT THE TRIBUTES every seven years since they lost the war. They were sacrifices, human flesh to feed the half man, half bull that was the Minotaur. By some twist of fate, he was Ariadne's twin. It had never settled well that she had shared a womb with someone who liked to eat the flesh of people while they screamed. The guards threw Ariadne in with the tributes.

A man among the tributes approached her immediately. He visibly looked Ariadne up and down like he was deciding whether or not to buy her at the marketplace. He announced in an overly loud voice. "I am Prince Theseus, the crown prince of Athens and heir to the throne. My father is the god of the sea, Poseidon." His pedigree was no small thing, but the way he announced it loudly to her like she was hard of hearing made it lose most of its effect.

Introduction made, he tried to grab her ass. Ariadne smacked his hand away, but that didn't seem to deter him in the slightest. He wrapped an arm around her waist like a snake. He pivoted them around as a unit to face the room. Dejected and terrified tributes stared at their prince with burgeoning hope.

"None of you shall perish this night, nor will I allow this to happen again. For I will end this senseless system at its source. I will kill the monstrous Minotaur!"

The tributes all cheered, for varying values of cheer. One older girl stared at him with a flat expression and patted her hands together, making no sound at all. Her much younger brother beside her was wildly cheering and had jumped to his feet and had joined a few of the others chanting, "Prince Theseus!"

"When we return to Athens, I'll make you my bride." He told Ariadne confidently, despite her not even knowing her name or identity. There was a massive difference between taking a lover in the following of a god famous for drunken orgies and being the wife of a future king. A foreign wife and queen in a land her father had ravaged with war and routinely sentenced their youth to slaughter, no less.

Theseus was an idiot. A horny one, given the way his hand once more dipped down and caressed her ass. Ariadne grabbed the offending hand in hers and did her best to distract him.

"I have a sword hidden in the labyrinth." She told him. Mostly because her father had threatened her with the labyrinth before and she hadn't wanted to be helpless should the worst happen.

The distraction worked and his face lit with eagerness, hands squeezing hers too hard. "Yes! Is there a way I can navigate the labyrinth?"

She looked away, biting her lip as she thought. She caught his gaze sharpening and focusing on her mouth. "I have a ball of thread. If you tie it to the start, then-"

"Then I'll be able to find my way back to the start!" Theseus cut her off and finished the sentence for her.

"I'll guide the rest of the tributes to a secret way out while you battle the Minotaur. You'll have to fight the guards once you return to the entrance of the Labyrinth. They will try to stop you from leaving or getting to the shipyard, dead Minotaur or not." Ariadne warned, heart aching as she realized there would be no way for her to get back to the camp before it moved.

"You're kidding. Why can't I go in first, alone? I could defeat the monster and return with no one else being in any danger." Theseus scowled at her as if he thought she could do anything about it. She might have been able to before she tried to leave, but that was then.

"They sent tributes into the labyrinth one per day, but only in the first year. Afterwards, the city council petitioned the king for him to release them all at once. They said the screaming going on for two weeks disrupted civic order." She informed him with a wince.

He grimaced, wide mouth twisting downward. "The screams of innocents inconveniencing them." Theseus spat to the side, and Ariadne couldn't blame him for his disgust.

"It's not the citizen's fault their king is the way he is." She told him with a heavy sigh. "I will guide the others out safely as I can. Tell them to obey me or they risk death. The labyrinth is full of deadly traps." She fibbed slightly. There were traps, but they deactivated on the night tributes were sent in. Her father called it enrichment to make sure the tributes lasted longer for the Minotaur. The confusing nature of the labyrinth itself kept all who went in lost until the Minotaur hunted them down. The beast never tried to escape when it still had live prey, after all.

Theseus didn't ask how she knew how to escape or navigate the labyrinth. He just nodded and then he kissed her. While Ariadne was still in shock, he said, "I will speak to them." He left to speak to the tributes on the other side of the large waiting chamber, not waiting for a response.

She touched her mouth gingerly. It had felt like he was trying to claim her. Like she was a thing he could have. To own. The way he thrust his tongue inside her mouth and probed at her without her consent made her scrub her lips futilely to get the invasive sensation off.

He was planning on doing that to her again. Ariadne had the feeling he would say he was claiming his 'prize'. If his dick felt as violating as his tongue had inside her... She shuddered and vowed to get him to find her unappealing enough to let her go.

Going from the prisoner of one man to another wasn't a pleasant prospect.

"What do you mean, you're taking part of my thread?" Theseus demanded, "That's supposed to guide me through the labyrinth!"

Ariadne pointed to the youngest child, who had started crying when the realization he had to go into the labyrinth sunk in. It was the boy that had been jumping up and dawn, chanting the prince's name after his speech. "Do you really resent sharing the thread so that they won't get lost and die alone in the labyrinth, monster or not?"

Theseus had finally subsided after that, stalking away to brood against a wall and stare meaningfully into the unlit labyrinth before them. The heavy metal gates had torches welded into their holders that lit only the entrance to the labyrinth.

She couldn't imagine what the sobbing boy's family had done to get a child less than ten sent to be killed by the Minotaur. His sister, holding his hand, was just this side of fully grown. Ariadne couldn't imagine how Athens could bear to send anyone at all. There wouldn't even be bodies to send home. There never had been.

Daedalus had been the one who to design and oversee the production of the labyrinth. He had felt responsible for the senseless tragedies taking place. So he had been the one to retrieve the pitiful remains of the tributes, risking encounters with the hopefully sated Minotaur. He buried them with coins from his own money, ensuring their passage to the other side of the river Styx into the afterlife.

He did that for two sets of tributes until he got caught doing so by the King's personal guards. He had escaped the King's personal savage beating alive, but would forever walk with a limp like his patron god.

Seven years later, after the next batch of tributes died, Daedalus's son and apprentice Icarus just buried the coins for them, with no bodies. He did so with a brief prayer for their souls to cross the river Styx peacefully. It might not count without their bodies to carry their payment for the ferryman, but at least it was more than not trying anything at all. Ariadne hoped the ferryman of the river had mercy on the tributes souls and granted them passage, despite the unorthodox method of payment.

Shortly after that, Icarus died during his and Daedalus's desperate flight from the country. His body had never been retrieved from the sea where he had drowned. Ariadne had followed his example and buried coins for Icarus to cross over with a prayer.

There had been no tributes in the seven years since. If any of them heading into the Labyrinth died this night, there was no one left to bury coins. It would be a long hundred year wait on the banks of the Styx for passage to the peace of Asphodel Meadows.

The tributes followed her silently, clinging to one another.

The traps had been disabled, making their winding passage in the pitch darkness almost easy. "I thought there were traps in here?" Whispered one of the braver ones from behind Ariadne's lead.

"The traps were removed so that nothing interferes with the Minotaur's hunt." Ariadne spoke before realizing she should have kept silent. Now committed, she continued, "Several of the previous group of sacrifices committed suicide that way." She was silent a moment, the memory of their bodies overwhelming her briefly. "That displeased the king."

Several of the sacrifices had a few choice words about that.

"And you just lead people in to die horrifically?" A belligerent voice from the line spoke up as they approached the last wall. "How are you any better than him?"

"I ran away to avoid doing just that." Ariadne said tiredly. "I got caught. Notice me being in here with you rather than out there giving out directions? My father doesn't like anyone."

The discontented murmuring went quiet after that, but Ariadne didn't believe that meant it would be gone forever. Hopefully, their obedience would last long enough for all of them to make it out of the labyrinth alive.

"Now everyone, take off your clothes." She ordered when she found the notch in the wall she was looking for. The shrieks were more manly than feminine, which was amusing. "Unless one of you wants to stay behind and be minus an arm?" No one said anything, and Ariadne realized how strange her order was from their perspective.

She explained, "I need something to trigger this trap. It will squeeze whatever is put in it and lift the wall, but only briefly and not very high, so we will have to be fast."

"Here." A girl handed her a wad of clothing. "I'm dedicating myself to Hestia after this shit. I don't care if anyone sees me naked."

Hearing this, the rest of the male tributes hand Ariadne their clothes without grumbling. She made a large compressed roll of clothes. "Ready?"

She waited for their affirmative noises and shoves the bundle in the hole as hard as she could. The wall rumbled and lifted, the full moon spilling light into the dark labyrinth as bright as day. The painfully young tributes sprung into action and rolled out under the grinding, slowly lifting wall. They went out one after another in quick succession.

When Ariadne was the only one left, she stopped pushing the bundle into the wall sconce and the wall slams down like a striking sword. There was no chance for her to even attempt to escape. She sighed and sagged against the stone wall, beginning to shake with adrenaline and fear, sliding down until she was kneeling. After a few minutes, she caught her breath and got up, wiping her tears away.

Either Theseus would meet her back at the entrance, or she would follow the thread to him. If he was dead, she would steal the sword off his body and kill her way out. It was more likely that either the Minotaur or the guards would kill her, but she would try.

ARIADNE made it to the entrance only moments before the Prince Theseus returned. He carried the Minotaur's bull head by the ear. Blood still dripped quickly from its mangled stump of a neck, pooling on the floor and hot against her bare feet. A dark part of her mind reminded her that's she was looking at her twin's decapitated head. She brushed the uncomfortable thought aside, along with the angry, accusing stare of the head.

Theseus dropped the head and pressed her against the wall, mouth once more on her. This time his blood covered hands were digging under her dress, dragging feverishly on her underclothes. Ariadne shoved him back, pulse pounding hard enough she could barely hear her own protest.

"There are guards!" She hissed, trying to cover her shaking. "They patrol to make sure no one escapes. If they catch you off guard like that, they'll kill you."

This common sense seemed to cool his ardor. He nodded, sweaty hair sticking to his forehead. "You're right. Let's get out of here." He picked up the head as large as her torso one handed with apparent ease and brushed past her.

Ariadne swallowed, closing her eyes at the thought of being alone on a ship with him, and then took a breath and followed.

# Chapter 3

ARIADNE HADN'T EVER really liked Phaedra before, but was quickly changing her mind. Her sister had forced her way onto the Athenian ship by sheer ego and ambition.

"If there's going to be a queen of Athens, it's going to be me." Phaedra sneered at her, tossing her silky hair over her shoulder.

Ariadne quietly found a corner of the ship to rest near the dozing tributes. She hunkered down by a coil of rope, hoping she was out of sight of Theseus.

Phaedra moved up to the prince, cutting him the rest of the way out of Ariadne's line of sight. "Oh, Theseus, you're so brave!" She plastered herself against his torso, shooting a dirty look over her shoulder. When she didn't see anyone, she buried her face in the bloody, dirty chest of a flattered looking Theseus.

Mentally wishing them the best, Ariadne tried to sleep.

THEY docked on an island in the middle of the night, tucking the ship into a hidden cove to hide from their pursuers. Dawn broke, pale light washing the long beach in pastels and soft edges.

Ariadne disembarked onto the island to avoid being alone with Theseus, despite his apparent distraction with her sister. She helped gather fresh water with the sailors and ate breakfast with the tired men.

The wine was terrible, but their food was more than passable. She certainly wasn't a master of making delicious wine, so tried not to judge them for the terrible tasting wine. It was better than what she had made and offered to Dionysus, after all.

ARIADNE woke up with a hammer pounding the inside of her head, ears ringing with a sound she couldn't place. She sat upright and almost fell over; the ground lurched under her.

Something was bothering her. What was it?

It was too quiet. The sailors had been loud. Even when exhausted, they had been constantly talking about their brave, heroic prince.

No one was on the beach. Ariadne turned her head slowly, vision swimming. There was no boat, or ship either. The sea stretched in front of the beach, empty but for a distant storm on the water.

It took several minutes for Ariadne to understand what had happened. They dumped her. They left her on the beach. She leaned back on the fishy smelling sand, closing her eyes against the brightness of the sun.

It was probably for the best, she told herself. Better than marrying Theseus and his octopus hands. She fell back asleep, the sun baking heat into her like a blanket.

ARIADNE dreamed of her lover. Lost lover now, she supposed. It wasn't like Dionysus was going to hunt down a singular mortal from a two-night fling, and finding gods was like finding a diamond on a beach. Possibly rarer.

But she dreamed of him. The way he cradled her head in his lap and brushed a gentle hand over her face. He picked her up and carried her close to his chest for a long time. The wind whipped against her partially numb face. It felt like they were going up, higher and higher, into the sky.

Perhaps she would see Icarus. He had flown into the sky. Wasn't he there still? The memory returned slowly. Icarus had fallen, wings melted and mangled. Abruptly, Ariadne was falling too.

ARIADNE woke with a start, jerking upright before her mind was fully awake. The sensation of falling still clung to her, tingling her nerves from head to toe.

"Whoa there, you're safe now." A dark man with an infinitely gentle demeanor got up from his desk, setting down his papers. He wore the clothes of a wealthy doctor, subtle designs made from fine linens draped generously over broad shoulders.

She glanced around the room. There was only a bed. The desk he had been sitting at had vanished. The window showed only open cloudless sky despite it being near the rainy season. "Where am I?"

"You're on Olympus." The doctor told her, pulling up a chair next to her bed that also hadn't existed prior to that moment.

Ariadne eyed him cautiously. "I'm listening."

"You believe me. Good." The doctor looked relieved. "That will make things easier." Ariadne didn't tell him this place was so obviously other that it was a dwelling of the gods or she was dead.

"Right. You were brought here with an... shall we say, advanced case of poisoning. Possibly accidental." He added in a hopeful tone. His face fell at her pained expression.

"Right. Well, I cured the poisoning. You'll be fine." He finished deliberately cheerful, teeth almost bared.

Ariadne went for the basics. "Why am I on Olympus?"

He stared at her. She stared back. He coughed, breaking eye contact. "Your lover?" He suggested gingerly, then nodded firmly. "Yes, you can ask your lover that."

Ariadne dearly hoped he meant Dionysus. If he meant the king of the gods, she was jumping out of that window, painful stop at the end or not. That fool vaporized lovers by accident. Case in point, Dionysus's mother.

"When?" Ariadne prodded.

"You don't have any further questions?" He sounded plaintive.

He had saved her life. She could be courteous even if she was desperately wondering what was going on. "What's your name?"

The god of doctors tells her his name. "Asclepius."

"Thank you." She told him. "I appreciate not being dead. Or in horrible pain." Asclepius practically glowed at the minimal praise. Emboldened, she went further. "Speaking of lovers, do you have anything to prevent pregnancy?"

He blinked, reached into his robe and pulled out a bundle of tiny pills and handed it to her. "This is the mix for immortal couple's contraceptives. Massive overkill for a mortal, of course, but given you're involved with a fertility deity, it might be better to be safe than sorry. Side effects are permanent infertility after more than a month of use." Asclepius informs her, tone brisk and professional. "Take one by mouth per day. You can chew, swallow or let it dissolve in your mouth. It won't affect how it works."

"Permanent infertility." Ariadne repeated. He nodded. She smiled and tucked the bag into her dress pocket. "Awesome."

"I'm always happy to prevent unwanted children." Asclepius told her with a proud smile.

A man walked into the room. To her relief, it was Dionysus. "You're awake!" He said as he flung himself on her, arms around her neck.

She hugged him back, breathing in the scent of flowers and the faint tang of wine. They both stayed like that for a long while, reveling in the warmth and presence of each other. Asclepius coughed awkwardly and left the room, the door closing with a quiet click.

"You found me," Ariadne breathed into his neck. "I didn't think..." She pressed her face into the curve of his shoulder.

Dionysus pulled back to look at her. "You didn't think what?" He asked, green eyes faintly luminescent.

"I didn't think you would even look." She admitted to him, amazed that he had. "I know that I'm certainly only one of many lovers for you. We had fun but-" She gave him a curious look, "I can't imagine it was enough to stand out for you."

Dionysus gave her a quirk of the lips that might've been a smile. "True. But you are my lover." The wine god said possessively, settling in on top of her heavily. "Mine. Not some upstart little demigod's wife." he added, eyes narrowed in such a way to leave them looking sharp. The winged eyeliner certainly added to the impression.

"My sister is the one you need to thank, then. She was all over Theseus." Ariadne grinned.

Dionysus winced. "Your sister is the one that drugged the wine."

"Then the poisoning was definitely an accident. Phaedra is quite good at manipulating men, but not measuring and numbers by a long shot." Ariadne told him with a snort.

"A little is good, but a lot is better?" Dionysus guessed and shook his head at her agreement.

"Listen, Ariadne. Mortals aren't allowed on Olympus."

# Chapter 4

HE CONTINUED, "ASCLEPIUS is a sucker for a mortal, so he won't say anything. But I'll need to disguise you."

Ariadne tilted her head to the side and smirked. "To get me off?"

Dionysus leered at her. "I will definitely get you off. But I was thinking, if you're alright with wearing a disguise, you could stay up here, with me."

Ariadne didn't want to misunderstand that he was offering. "You mean to have sex?"

He shrugged, flipping a hand back and forth. "That too. Have some fun together."

"I'd love to." She smiled at him, feeling shy. "I was going to go with the camp anyway, before they caught me." Ariadne ran a hand through his long hair, curling it around a finger and gently tugging it. "Sticking closer to you is hardly a hardship."

The smile she received was blinding, and he suddenly pulled her to her feet. "This is going to sting a bit," Dionysus warned her before the sensation of bee stings covered her skin from head to toe.

She barely had time to yelp in pain before it stopped. Dionysus propped a materialized mirror in front of her. In the mirror, a male satyr with her face and wearing her dress looked back in shock. She had small horse ears that were almost lost in the fall of her hair. She twisted around and saw the tip of a horse's tail was barely visible under the edge of her skirt.

She looked away from the mirror and down at herself. She saw her normal self, no animal or gender changes. "How does this work?"

"Magic." Dionysus told her solemnly before he cackled at her expression. "Nah, it just makes you look and feel like the image I constructed. To everyone but you, that is."

"Even you?" He nodded, and she ventured to ask, "Why am I male?"

"My maenads are lovely, lovely women, but they are also mortal and thus utterly forbidden to be up here." Dionysus pointed out with a brief sigh. "Satyrs are both male, immortal, and always found in my company. The perfect disguise." He finished with relish, tweaking her tail and making her jump at the phantom sensation.

She swatted his hand away from her tail. Curiosity overwhelms her and she asked, cheeks heating, "How does this work for sex, if I'm the only one to see or touch my real self?"

Dionysus smile widened, showing his teeth. He purred, "I was hoping you would ask that."

⸻ ◉ ⸻

DIONYSUS introduced her as Ampelos, his new companion. No one batted an eye at this or the fact the male satyr wore women's clothes.

No one really looked at her much at all. Apparently, satyrs were below the give a shit threshold of the more powerful gods. Even the lesser ones trying to seem more powerful didn't give her a second glance. She heard one god tell another that 'Ampelos' was Dionysus's newest accessory in front of her face.

On the other hand, Dionysus was quite popular. He dragged her everywhere with him, seemingly for the enjoyment of her company. He held her tightly during the night like a teddy bear. Ariadne loved it, but was worried about how she would sleep when she eventually lost his attention. All mortals were only temporary to the gods, a fact she saw reinforced the longer she was on Olympus.

The sheer desperation in Dionysus's frequently too tight sleeping hugs worried her. So she didn't struggle to break free unless he was actually impeding her breathing. She tried stroking his hair and back gently, and that helped with the fierceness of his grip.

But what helped most of all, she learned by accident.

"Did you have a nightmare?" Dionysus asked her, sleep slurring his speech as he petted her hair gently.

"Yes." Ariadne admitted, feeling her fingers dig into his flesh as she pulled him and his heat closer to her.

He hummed sleepily and continued stroking her hair. "Do you want to talk about it?"

She did. She didn't. "Maybe." She conceded.

He dragged his nails across her scalp and goosebumps ran down her arm. "That felt amazing. Do it again." She ordered with a happy sigh.

"Tell me about your nightmare." Dionysus countered.

Ariadne huffed, but conceded the head scratching was worth it. "Fine." She took a deep breath. "I dreamed Theseus got me pregnant. And that after he abandoned me on that stupid island, I died giving birth to twins. Alone. In the dark. During a horrible storm." She didn't mention the agony of birth pains from her monstrous children tearing themselves free from her womb by eating it and each other.

The head scratches stopped for a moment, then resumed. "Well. That is definitely a nightmare. I'll give you that. But, no worries, you are safe and sound here with me." The god sounded especially smug at the last part. His fingers began gently combing out her sleep braid into what would be a nightmare of knots in the morning.

She relaxed and dozed as he made a mess of her hair. She held onto him, feeling safe and cared for in his warm embrace. The sun began letting in watery predawn light through the huge open windows in the room. She fell back asleep as the last of the dark faded.

AFTER that, Ariadne realized holding Dionysus tightly made him relax. The whole time she held him after a nightmare, he relaxed his grip into something that was cuddly instead of the previously borderline uncomfortable grip. She attempted to glue herself to his side whenever she woke up at night.

She wasn't sure if he even knew he did it, so she never mentioned it. Gods, and more to the point, men could be delicate about their weak points being perceived.

As she learned about his history through blatant eavesdropping, more became harshly clear about the sources of his idiosyncrasies.

Child gods were not much less powerful than fully grown gods. But their control was that of children. Dionysus was not just the god of wine and parties. He was also a god of madness. One who had grown up in the mortal world, where they were so much more fragile than the immortals of Olympus.

The specifics of what happened were never even hinted at, apparently harsh enough even the immortal gods shied away from talking about. But the fact it happened multiple times, and repeatedly destroyed his life, came through loud and clear.

Apparently, the stories that Hera took exception to her husband's bastard and destroyed his life were lies. Lies told to spare a child the horror of knowing what had happened had been partially his fault. That struck Ariadne as stupid and unintentionally cruel. If Dionysus didn't know it was him, how could he learn to prevent it from happening again and again? He couldn't.

The harvest goddess Demeter apparently had the same thoughts as Ariadne, because she had taught him control. Given her experience with her mad father, she was probably one of the best choices for the job.

⸻ ◈ ⸻

ARIADNE leaned over as she handed Dionysus a fresh bunch of figs to snack on and said in a low tone. "Is it because I'm a satyr?"

He followed her glance to nearby, where a couple nymphs were giggling at a rude story about the king of the gods that was inappropriately detailed. It was likely accurate too, given his reputation.

Dionysus grinned at her, face open and full of mischief. "You haven't figured it out then? They don't think you speak the language."

Ariadne blinked at him. She spoke the Titan language more than Olympian, but they were close enough she was picking it up quickly. But then, both were languages used exclusively by the gods and chosen immortals of Olympus. Her mother was the daughter of a Titan and had passed the knowledge down to her children, occasionally against their will. A mark of prestige Ariadne had thought, but was coming to wonder if her mother had just missed her homeland.

She leaned in to kiss his cheek and ask, "What about you then? Why do people speak so openly around you, when you do speak their language?"

He pulled her onto his lap for a full kiss, lazy and affectionate. He pulled back to answer the question after several long, distracting minutes. "A mix. I'm always drunk, full of bad ideas that are too fun to say no to and, well. This is what most of them see when they talk to me." Dionysus gives her his dopiest expression.

While adorable, to the unwitting it gave the impression he was not the most intelligent person. He probably had more blackmail on the entirety of Olympus than personal messenger to bullshit Hermes did.

Ariadne kissed him again, before she licked his lower lip and pulled back. "Do you think I could pull that off?"

Dionysus considered. "No, you have such sharp eyes, it wouldn't work. But too foreign to understand..." He waggled his eyebrows at her.

Ariadne frowned at him, brows knitting together. "Is that an immortal thing?" She asked hesitantly, looking down at him through her eyelashes. Her unsure voice was at odds with the confidence her hand was moving across his chest.

Dionysus grinned, sharp and pleased. "Exactly."

# Chapter 5

ARIADNE HAD A LOT OF fun on Olympus as Ampelos the satyr. She had a lot of fun back in the mortal realm, too, reveling in wearing her own skin under the heat of the sun. She took to going topless, with only her loose hair covering her breasts. It drew fewer glances than she feared, the festivals always seeming to have people in various states of undress.

Her lover frequently eschewed clothes entirely, and the ones he wore slipped and slid, showing more than they concealed. The only exception was when he dressed as a woman, like the first day they had met.

It was wild, freeing and when not exhilarating, oddly relaxing. Dancing, drinking, laughing and singing were fun. But so were the long slow treks from place to place, winding flowers in everyone's hair, and chatting idly with people as they passed through.

Ariadne looked, but didn't find anyone who appealed to her to take as a lover besides the one she already had. It would have been smart to plan for the future when she would no longer be favored by Dionysus. To take another lover and avoid the pain of being alone.

But Ariadne's brain dribbled right out of her ears without fail when she made eye contact with Dionysus. Giving up before she even tried to find a mortal lover, she settled into watching Dionysus seduce those who caught his eye. She found she rather enjoyed watching, with the way his eyes flicked up, found her watching and gave her a secret smile.

He always took her back with him to Olympus when he left the mortal realm, even if they hadn't been lovers in weeks. She'd ask why, but it was obvious at that point he was frequently lonely in the realm of the gods. His sleeping grip tightened to the point of painful when they were there. She suspected being there either brought up bad memories or there were people there that had hurt him. Ariadne wasn't sure what she could do besides be there for him.

They were sitting outside under the low hanging canopy of a fig tree that shielded them from the scorching summer sun. Ariadne finally asked him, "Why don't you have sex with people here?"

Dionysus took her as a lover in the mortal world infrequently, but on Olympus they were lovers only rarely. He touched very few people at all in Olympus.

Dionysus cracked open an eye from where he was using her lap as a pillow. "What brings this on?"

"You don't seem very happy here. Not like your usual self. Repressed." She frowned down at him and used her finger to fix his smudged eyeliner. He allowed it, closing his eyes under her ministrations.

"There's not much here I find joy in." He didn't open his eyes.

"Can you make a party?" She suggested, hesitant and sure it was a bad idea to suggest, but not sure why.

"They would love that." Her lover said bitterly. "They always love my parties."

Ariadne caught the strange inflection. "You don't think they love you."

Dionysus opened both eyes and looked at her, silent. She sighed and stroked his cheek and pinched the tip of his nose. "I can't fix that. Give me a problem I can fix." She mock scowled at him.

His smile is mocking and strange. "You don't want to love me enough for all of them?"

"I grew up with a family that didn't care for me either. Even you can't make that pain any less. I doubt that I have that ability for you, either." Ariadne admitted, staring at his nose to avoid the intensity of his gaze. With his powers rippling underneath his skin like lightning, his glowing green eyes were eerie. "I try." She admitted and closed her eyes, feeling foolish.

He was her lover, but he was also a god. She wasn't anyone special to him and he held powers that would likely kill her if she even saw them unveiled, much like how his mother had died. The legend of Semele, the woman who bore a god and looked at the true form of another was a quiet one. But within the following of Dionysus, it was a frequently told tale.

She swallowed and tried something dangerous. "Your birth mother... have you ever went to the Underworld and spoken to her?"

When she opened her eyes, he was looking at her like she slapped him with a live fish. She pulled her hands back from him and looked away. "I don't mean to upset you."

Dionysus pulled himself upright and gripped her hands. "No, no, no. Don't do that. Don't be afraid of me." Ariadne looked at him. He demanded worship and respect as a god, but also wanted to be treated as a man. She wasn't sure he realized those things were mutually exclusive of each other. "Please." His voice cracked.

Ariadne rested her forehead against his. Dionysus surged up and rubbed his cheek against hers like the large cats he sometimes took the form of. "I won't hurt you." He promised. "Not you. Never you."

"Oh." Ariadne managed, stunned by his fervor.

"Do you," When he was satisfied she wasn't flinching, he began, "Do you think it would help? To talk to her. My mother, Semele."

Ariadne realized he was asking her this. He was seriously asking her if talking to his dead mother would make his struggle with loneliness and being accepted by the other gods easier. She mentally flailed.

"I think," She licked her lips. "That talking to her would give you closure. Possibly blackmail, depending if she remembers what your father's true form looked like." She added thoughtfully, hoping that bit didn't get her in trouble down the line. His father was the king of the gods. But Zeus had also shown his very pregnant lover his true form as a god and killed her instantly, so screw him.

Technically, only three gods went to the Underworld and came back. Hecate was a goddess with powers over the lingering dead. Hermes did as well, but as a god who delivered things that also occasionally included lost souls. Persephone was the queen of the Underworld. But before that, she had been associated with her mother Demeter, goddess of the harvest and food crops.

"Your powers are strong with plants, so going to the Underworld in the winter wouldn't be completely unheard of." She added, extremely hesitant at giving advice on something she had very little knowledge of.

Dionysus's expression gleamed with a manic excitement. "Blackmail, huh?" He kissed her cheek and bit her illusory horse ear playfully, cackling at her yelp. "What would I do without you?" He told her with a cheerful grin, melancholy mood gone like a cloud over the sun.

Ariadne wasn't sure what she would do without him, either. It was probably something she should be more worried about.

⚬

IT did not entirely shock Ariadne when Dionysus went to the Underworld. It surprised her that he took her advice, but not too much. He clearly had a lot of unresolved feelings that had been with him for a long while. Since childhood, she was assuming.

What did shock her into confusion was when he dropped her off with the goddess Demeter while he went on his quest. Dionysus didn't stay long enough to explain, hurrying off to catch a ride with a patiently waiting Persephone. The air was already losing heat, and they had only left minutes ago.

Ariadne turned from staring at the stubbornly empty horizon to the harvest goddess standing next to her. "I have no idea why I am here." She admitted.

Demeter snorted. "You sure about that?" She continued watching where the chariot had faded into the distance as the darkness of night swallowed it. "You don't strike me as the stupid type."

Ariadne tried to figure that out and then gave it up as a lost cause. "I know that I'm relatively favored as Dionysus's lover, but I thought he was going to leave me with the traveling bands or even at one of his temples. I don't know why he left me here." She repeated with a bit more explanation, hoping to get one in return.

"Relatively favored? Girl, you convinced a god of the vibrancy of life to go to the realm of the dead willingly. Not even my Persephone did that before her marriage." Demeter told her flatly.

Ariadne was shaking her head before Demeter finished. "Dionysus wanted to meet his mother." She corrected, but quietly, because she was arguing with a goddess. Ariadne tried not to focus too much on the fact Demeter had seen no problem with killing all of humanity at one point. "I think he had forgotten that he could, since they accepted him as a god."

Demeter finally looked away from the horizon and gave her a measuring look. "I suppose there is that."

But she didn't tell Ariadne why she was there.

# Chapter 6

DIONYSUS CAME BACK at the end of the winter, noticeably paler and calmer. He came back with a woman who was breathtakingly beautiful and looked like his sister. Ariadne ached suddenly for the loss of her twin and the possibility their fates could have been anything but what they were.

"This is Ariadne, mother." Dionysus said, fairly glowing under the more solemn expression of his mother. His conspicuously not dead mother. Beside him, Persephone gave Demeter and Ariadne both a hopeful look, glancing back at Semele pointedly.

Ariadne had come around to Demeter's don't ask, don't tell policy over the winter. She was seeing the benefits of it. She was also desperate to get away from canning preserves.

Semele raised an elegant eyebrow. "I wasn't aware you picked favorites among your followers."

Dionysus looked surprised. "I don't. Ariadne's not one of my followers." This gained Ariadne a sharp look from two goddesses and a former corpse. "She's a lot of fun." He finished lightheartedly, diffusing some of the tension.

"Fun. I'll tell you fun. I've spent so long canning and pickling things the next time I see your dick, I'm liable to pickle it by habit." Ariadne gritted out with a pleasant smile.

"She's actually pretty good at it." Demeter praised.

Persephone asked with a laugh, "Have you two had to pickle many genitals this winter?"

Ariadne gave the queen of the underworld a thousand-yard stare. "Just mine. Your mother may be very attractive, but I suspect she only has sex to make babies. I had cobwebs in my underwear." She finished plaintively, making Dionysus laugh, and sweep her into a possessive, groping hug.

Ariadne hadn't been kidding. There had been cobwebs in her underwear as spiders had laid a horrific sized egg sack in a pair that was squashed in the drawer's corner.

Demeter grimaced. "I admit, that was unnerving, even for me." She said under her breath to her daughter, who looked delighted and intrigued.

Dionysus pulled back from the hug to tug a strand of her hair free from her braid and study it. "Are you going silver?" He asked seriously before mock gasping and covering his mouth with his free hand. "How long was I gone?"

Ariadne's stomach sunk to her toes. She was going silver. Hopefully, the early silver hair was a side effect of her mother's linage. Her mother went silver young as well, but her mother was also married and an immortal. Ariadne wasn't young enough, marriageable or anything else a woman was supposed to be. Not any longer. She failed that stage of her life and thus, everyone after it. Nailed it.

Semele rolled her eyes and reached over to swat her son's hand. "Don't make her self-conscious. Very few women are immortal, but many are beautiful nonetheless." She smiled at Ariadne, who could suddenly see the resemblance between the two of them. Their genuine smiles were identical.

Unfortunately, Ariadne's hormones kicked in and remind her that a beautiful woman was smiling at her. Semele's visual similarity to Dionysus dressed as a woman just made it worse. Ariadne immediately avoided eye contact with the other woman.

"Sorry, sorry." He apologized, dropping Ariadne's silver hair to plant a kiss on her forehead before whipping out a flower crown from one of his ridiculously oversized dress pockets. He settled it on her head, tongue poking out from the corner of his mouth.

Dionysus had made her a crown of asphodel. From the Underworld. Ariadne chose to be flattered instead of nervous at the implication she would die soon.

"Thank you."

He turned to his mother and smirked. "See, I told you she would like it."

Semele gave Ariadne a confused look. "Why do you thank him for that? It's flowers from the world of the dead."

Dionysus didn't give other people flower crowns at all and it made her feel special. Ariadne shrugged and defended herself as best she could, without revealing her true reasoning. "Flowers are pretty. No place is untouched by life, just as no place is untouched by death. Pretending it doesn't just sucks the joy out of what time you do have." She'd learned that one with the labyrinth and the days there that never seemed to end.

Semele just shook her head. "He has you wrapped around his finger."

Ariadne grinned, feeling a surge of wickedness. "I wouldn't say it's his finger that I wrap around."

<hr>

THEY stopped by the traveling camp, spreading the word of what Dionysus had done. Ariadne still couldn't quite believe it, despite seeing the formerly dead woman daily for several weeks. No one had ever come back from the Underworld. No one.

Well, except Sisyphus, but that had been trickery, and he had paid the price for that. Still was, likely enough in the depths of Tartarus. Semele, on the other hand would soon be made an immortal. Dionysus would never lack for a trusted face on Olympus again.

Semele was so very different from her son. The wild, untamed edge that always lurked under the surface of him was absent from her. Dionysus played stupid exceptionally well, whereas Semele was almost entirely inscrutable.

Even when Dionysus revealed his plan to have Semele made immortal, his mother merely smiled mysteriously. Ariadne still couldn't get a read on what the woman thought of her. Semele's eyes were frequently on her, but she never confronted Ariadne over anything.

Except once.

Semele had cornered her one early morning after Ariadne had a bath. The rest of the camp still slept, thoroughly hungover from the previous nights festivities. Ariadne had realized with some bemusement she couldn't remember the last time she had a hangover.

"Dionysus sleeps around." Semele noted in her usual neutral tone of voice as she settled in, sitting next to Ariadne on the log. No hello or other form of greeting, just straight to the point. Except not asking anything directly. How the other woman knew about her son's sexual activities, Ariadne wasn't sure. She was placing her bets on the ramped up gossip that came with a divine miracle.

She waited for Semele to actually ask a question. She had learned by watching and falling victim to it herself that Semele would simply give no response and let the other person babble on. Ariadne's hair slowly unknotted with her patient strokes of the brush as she waited. She had grown tempted to shear it all off, but it would be difficult to hide her growing streak of silver that way.

Semele inclined her head, as if Ariadne had said something instead of giving the woman a blank stare. "Does it bother you?"

Ariadne considered this. She had of course done so before, but given that this was Dionysus's mother newly back from corpseville, it gave the question new weight. "I want him to be happy." She said finally.

"But does it bother you?" Semele pressed, turning to face Ariadne more directly on the wide log next to the tranquil stream.

"Why do you care?" Ariadne returned, not quite comfortable revealing her feelings to someone not her lover.

"Because you have no friends to ask you to have you think of yourself." The woman responded promptly and Ariadne dropped her brush. She stared at the other woman and felt the strong urge to burst into abrupt tears. No one had ever told her to think of herself. Only of her parents, their family honor, her duties, then later on only of her lover.

She swallowed the tight knot in her throat and picked up her hairbrush. "I love him, more than I should, I know. Gods are..." Ariadne sighed, unwilling to say fickle and violent and frequently uncaring of the mortal lives as more than amusements. "You understand."

"I do." Semele agreed dryly.

Ariadne bit her lip. "I could leave him if I truly wanted to. If I found someone who would be faithful, marry me, that sort of thing. But I like him as a person, not just a lover." He was, to Ariadne's surprise, her friend. It had never even crossed her mind after she had first found out he was a god. Yet, here she was.

Semele repeated her question for a third time. "Does it bother you?"

Ariadne was quiet for so long that her hair started drying. "Yes. I feel replaceable." She admitted, feeling as if she had committed blasphemy. She took a breath. "That's good though." She told herself.

Semele's eyebrows raised at her statement.

"It would be stupid to forget it." Ariadne reminded the older mentally but younger physically woman. It was strange to realize all over again that Semele would be immortal soon. She felt like they were switching roles, almost. Ariadne was aging and Semele going to Olympus.

Semele reached out and smoothed Ariadne's unruly hair out of her face. "You undervalue yourself. My son cares for you deeply."

"No, I can do the math. How many mortals make it to Olympus and become immortal? How many have faithful partners? How many are loved and then set aside as they age?" Ariadne pulled open the thick trail of her hair to show Semele her growing streak of silver. The light caught it and it began glittering madly in the morning sunlight.

Semele sat back, lips pressed tightly together, but did not argue.

"My suggestion is once you reach Olympus, find yourself a woman for a lover. They have a better record for pleasing women, in every way." Ariadne advised her wryly.

"Dionysus told you, then." Semele sighed, rubbing her forehead. "I do not know how he expects this to work. Back from the dead or not, Zeus does not hand out immortality like candy and most especially to his former lovers. In front of his wife, no less."

"Guilt trip." Ariadne summarized instantly. "After the awful nightmare of Dionysus's childhood, he's got a lot of emotional blackmail credit. There is also the rumor Zeus felt bad about the whole accidentally killing you thing." She finished awkwardly, realizing as she did Semele might be triggered by the mention of her death.

"No amount of emotional blackmail will soothe his wife." Semele pointed out with a shake of her head, seemingly unbothered. "He will please her in this matter first."

Ariadne paused. She thought about the way Dionysus clung to her in his sleep. "I wouldn't put any bets on that. By the way, I'm coming with you to Olympus. But not in the way you're used to seeing me..."

# Chapter 7

ARIADNE AS AMPELOS had to pick her jaw off the ground. Semele was not only made immortal, but Zeus also made her a goddess. Looking around, she realized the only other person as surprised at this was Semele herself. Or rather, she wasn't Semele any longer but Thyone. A minor goddess of the frenzies that were characteristic of the festivals of Dionysus's followers.

Ariadne cornered the new goddess alone as soon as she could the next day. There had been no chance the night before during the party that was thrown in Thyone and Dionysus's honor.

"If you find out what your being made into a goddess was about, please pass it on." She requested of the new goddess, passing her a glass of water.

Thyone only shook her head silently. Probably from the hangover, come to think of it. Oddly, she didn't seem immune to hangovers like Dionysus was and Ariadne had become.

Ariadne didn't get any answers in that direction. Thyone was as quietly regal and close lipped as her mortal self was. She did, on rare occasion, send Ariadne pitying looks.

Ariadne understood the new goddess felt bad for her. She would likely soon be passed over in favor of someone else, and Thyone had received her happy ending past all reasonable expectations of getting one. Ariadne knew that there would be no happy ending for her, not even a belated one like Thyone had received. Despite that, the pitying looks still pissed her off, and she took to avoiding the new goddess.

It was depressingly easy. Thyone consorted almost exclusively with women and her son was the only exception allowed in the gatherings. Satyrs were banned for always being horny and having poor impulse control. Or so Ariadne as Ampelos was told by a nervous nymph blocking the door to yet another gathering.

Since Dionysus spent at least half his time with his mother, this left Ariadne with a surprising amount of free time that had been previously occupied. She used it to brood and strike up a friendship with Silenus. He was a frequently drunk old satyr that had something to do with raising Dionysus, although no one spoke of how in detail. His childhood continued to be referred to in winces and insider references.

Silenus was kind and patient with her as he showed her how the wine on Olympus was made. "The gods can whip up their own any time, of course, but the rest of us get to make do with the old-fashioned way." He told her with a whiskery smile.

Then came the day the old satyr made her blood run cold. "I don't say this to be cruel, my child, but how long are you planning on disguising yourself? Such things cannot last forever."

Ariadne was wrist deep in the dirt, planting grape cuttings and sprayed dirt over them both when she recoiled. "W-what?" She stuttered before his words even registered with her higher brain functions.

He sighed and squatted next to her in the vineyard row to pat the upturned plant back down into the warm earth. "It's obvious to this old satyr that you're not a satyr at all. There are signs. But I don't know why you are risking Tartarus tricking the gods. They don't take kindly to this kind of thing." Silenus gave the ground one last pat and looked her in the eye, his tone grave. "And they will find out, eventually."

"Dionysus is the one who disguised me." She confessed, feeling her anxiety spike with the admission. "I don't have any talent with magic at all." Which galled her the longer she thought about it. Her mother and aunt were mighty users of magic. Her cousin Medea was rumored to be pants shitting powerful. Even her limp-wristed sister Phaedra could work up a glow like a dim moon when she was upset.

The Minotaur really had sucked up all the power in their shared womb. Or maybe she gave it to him so he could survive with his mutated body. Either way, there was no going back. Ariadne had no magic that she knew of.

Silenus looked sad. "Dionysus being the one to cast the disguise won't help you, lad. When things go bad, it's always the mortals that pay the price. I would have said something earlier, but with the hubbub of everything that was Thyone's arrival, it got away from me."

Ariadne thought of her ever widening silver streak. "I don't know what to do." She admitted with a sigh, running a dirty hand through her messy hair.

"Stay in the mortal realm." Silenus advised. "I've taught you enough you can find a place in any of my boy's traveling bands or if some royal catches your eye, you'd be a fine vintner."

She wrinkled her nose. "I've only been learning this a little more than a year. I know that I have a lot more to learn."

Silenus gave her a sly smile. "The mortal realm has much lower standards, you'll find."

She snorted, but smiled reluctantly. "Point." Ariadne inhaled the smell of fresh green leaves and wet turned earth, the sun warming her face.

Maybe it was time.

⊸●⊷

ARIADNE tried to talk to Dionysus before she left. She really did. But after the fourth time she entered a room, and he left it as soon as catching sight of her, she realized he was avoiding her. That was new. She did not know why, nor had the patience for such games.

She waited one last night in the room she shared with him. He didn't come back that night either.

So Ariadne wrote a note, awkward and frustrated that their true last words together would be him saying, "I'm going to go see my mother," and her distracted response of, "Tell her hello from me, will you?"

She wrote carefully, breathing slowly as to not let her jitteriness show in her handwriting. She wrote out how she tried to seek him out and failed, how she was worried she would be found out and punished, and how she was going back to the mortal realm.

Ariadne looked at what she wrote.

She scribbled over the note and ate it. Ashes could be reconstructed in Olympus, where everyone but her held magic like children's toys. The residents there had nothing but time to be breathtakingly nosy with anyone or anything remotely interesting. She wrote another note.

Had a lot of fun together! Going back to the mortal world.

Ariadne stared at it for long minutes before sighing and adding an achingly careful,

Goodbye.

⎯⎯◆⎯⎯

ARIADNE walked down the mountain, the warm summer morning fading into the cool of a predawn autumn morning within the space of minutes. The realm of the gods vanished behind her, and she couldn't help but feel the air was fresher.

It was also cold. But keeping track of the seasons on Olympus was tricky, since it changed only at the whim of the king. Time flowed slower there as well, which was part of why they had trouble connecting to mortals. Or so she suspected.

Ariadne made it to the base of the mountain by midday, sweaty with her exertions. She sat at the base of an olive tree and took a nap, not really thinking of anything but the warmth of the afternoon and the burning in her legs. She was definitely not acknowledging the suppressed tears that kept trying to press their way out.

She woke up to Dionysus standing in front of her, face creased with fury, her note crumpled in his clenched fist. His power flared around him, rippling the air like a heatwave.

"What. Is. This?" He hissed, hair radiating around him like a corona. He stepped forward to drop the crunched ball of paper into her lap like a dead mouse.

Ariadne wasn't sure why Dionysus was upset. It made a small part of her, hidden in the hurt from what she'd had to do, happy. But even it didn't dare whisper its quiet hope of love into words. She knew better, after all.

"I tried to talk to you." She said, squinting up at him. The sun was behind his head, crowning Dionysus with blinding light and shadowing his face all at once. "You kept leaving the room as soon as you saw me. I took the hint. You didn't want to talk to me."

Ariadne picked up the crumpled ball of paper and was suddenly at a loss for words and out of her depth. It was wet in spots. As if someone had cried on it. Gods didn't cry. They didn't. Not over easily replaceable mortals.

"I thought we were friends." Dionysus said coldly.

I thought you loved me back. The unspoken thought came at the same time he spoke. She wished that was what he had said, instead of her mind tricking her.

# Chapter 8

ARIADNE CUT HIM OFF before he could continue, not wanting to know more, her heart already experiencing pangs of burgeoning hope. "Of course we are! But if Silenus can see through my disguise, I didn't have much time before someone else less friendly found out."

Something passed across his face, impossible to make out in shadow. "Silenus?"

"He told me I would live longer if I got out while the charade held up." Ariadne sighed, smoothing out the wrinkled paper, fingers brushing the wet spots. There was no mistaking the golden tint for anything besides divine tears. "I never intended to hurt you." More to avoid further pain, really.

"I- I thought you wanted nothing to do with me." Dionysus suddenly sounded like an unsure man, and not an infuriated scorned god. The wrathful aura was gone, like it had never even existed. It had probably been the pain of rejection, wrapped up in the thin comfort of anger.

Ariadne set the paper aside and stood up, pulling him into a tight, slightly sweaty hug. "You are my friend. Always." She held him for long minutes before pulling back to look at him. His body was finally out of that awful dark shadow of power and the untouchable divine perfection was gone. His face was still wet, expression heartbreakingly hopeful under his smeared makeup.

"It would just be rather hard to be your friend as a smear on the floor of Olympus." She told him wryly with a smile.

He didn't smile back. "I would never let that happen to you."

She let her smile fade. "You can't control everything." She told him solemnly.

Dionysus stared at her wordlessly, eyelashes still wet with tears. Ariadne pulled him back into her arms for another hug. He slowly relaxed into it until he was limp in her arms. The sun beat down on them and eventually she pulled him under the tree to join her afternoon nap. He lay his head in her lap and interlaced his hands with hers.

Ariadne didn't sleep, chewing her lip as she ran her thumb over their joined hands. She had a problem. She had a big problem. Thyone who was former Semele was wrong. Ariadne had a friend, but she had stupidly forgotten that. Gods might treat their lovers with varying levels of care and then move on. But friends were almost universally treasured while they lived.

First and foremost, Dionysus was her friend. They may not have started that way, but it was what they had wound up as. Ariadne had forgotten that, buried under her secret desire to have him to herself, to be the center of his world as he was hers. Combined with her loneliness as Dionysus got to know his mother for the first time, her common sense had been overwhelmed. She forgot what she already had.

Ariadne was going to die. There was no way around that. She would have an eternity in the Underworld, probably wandering around without memory. Or maybe she would be eternal prey to her twin, the Minotaur. It would suit as punishment for leading innocents to their deaths and never trying to help until it was her neck on the line. She had dreamed about it often enough lately.

In comparison, her time alive was going to be short. Ariadne glanced down at the dozing god in her lap. Dionysus was going to live a long, long time. He had already been alone too long. His mother would be there for him, as she couldn't be during his childhood. Ariadne could only hope after she died the memory of their relationship wouldn't make him feel worse than before.

But she couldn't control that. What she could control was what she did with her time while she was alive. No matter how the thought of her wandering around after life and picking flowers while someone she cared about suffered alone pissed her off. What ate at her the most was that she wouldn't even be able to remember him after the traditional drinking of Lethe.

"I can feel you thinking." Dionysus muttered into her thigh, breath hot on her skin where her dress had ridden up. A green eye peered up at her through the hair spilled across his face.

"I am thinking, imagine that." Ariadne squeezed his hands with hers before pulling one free to run it through his hair. They stayed like this for long enough that she almost dozed off herself. All she could smell was the roses in his now crooked flower crown and the sun baked rock surrounding them.

"Why did you stop meeting my eyes when I took lovers at my revels?"

Ariadne's eyes popped open. He blinked sleepily up at her, patiently waiting.

"Why did you avoid me on Olympus?" She countered, embarrassed about her jealousy.

"I asked first." Dionysus pointed out reasonably enough, and had the gall to be smug about it. She recognized his expression from his terrible attempts at poker face when he tried to practice against her before entering the divine tournament. When he thought he was getting away with something, the skin around his eyes curved, matching the movement of his mouth.

Ariadne started slow, picking her words carefully as she thought them out. "It felt like a game when it first started. You would wander far and wide, but always come back and spend time with me. We would sit up the whole night talking and laughing. But then you quit talking to me as much, or touching me as your lover."

"When I brought mother back." Dionysus agreed.

"You didn't want me as a lover. You had replaced as your friend, too. That hurt." She stared dully up at the sun through the dappled leaves of the tree. "It wasn't fun to play the game anymore. It felt like I was watching from the outside of something I wanted but wasn't needed or wanted at."

"I'm sorry." The low words caught her by surprise, but he had completely buried his face in her lap now. She had nothing to gauge his sincerity but the muffled tone and the tight grip on her hands still holding his.

"Me too. I should have said something earlier." Ariadne admitted bitterly, thumping her head against the bark of the tree. An olive fell and smacked her on the head, making her yelp.

"Quit that." Dionysus rolled out of her lap to catch the back of her head with his hands, mirroring their first meeting. "You'll hurt yourself, Ariadne."

Their eyes met, brown and cat green. The moment hung between them. Dionysus leaned forward and pressed a soft kiss to her lips, chaste. He rested his forehead against hers, smudging his makeup onto her. He closed his eyes and swore quietly.

"I was avoiding you because- I didn't know, still don't know how to really- to talk about-" Dionysus cut himself off with a sigh, opening his eyes. Up close, she could see the starburst of darker green that surrounded his pupil and the pale yellow ring surrounding his iris.

"Is this something you don't have words for, don't know how to explain, or are not sure what you're trying to say?" Ariadne prodded gently, pushing her arms to surround his neck and lacing her hands together loosely.

Dionysus gave her a crooked smile and pressed a kiss to her nose. "You have the kindest heart." He deflected instead of answering.

"No, I'm not." She whispered to him, confessing her darkness in a cracking voice. "I would have left that labyrinth and never went back if I could have. I would have let my father slaughter countless children and thought only of how I was relieved to have escaped. I tried to."

Ariadne thought of her twin, the way blood dripped from his severed head in a hot pool at her feet. The begging and screaming of sacrifices not old enough to leave home alone led to slaughter. The ruins of wax wings washing up the shore.

He said nothing at first, pulling back and studying her. "It's not wrong for you to have fled from being a part of that evil. It was not your fault, nor your duty to stop what your father did." He finally spoke and pulled his hands up from cradling the back of her head to cup her cheeks.

Dionysus licked his lips slowly and asked carefully, "Do you feel you have to escape me?"

"I felt like I had to leave before you broke my heart by forgetting me entirely." She covered his hands with hers and didn't meet his eyes, staring instead at his glittering earrings. "I'm lonely on Olympus. Even with you. It's a place of gods and immortals, not 'base animal companions.'" She quoted.

"Who told you that?" He demanded sharply, leaning back on his heels, ferocious expression from earlier returning.

"Who didn't?" Ariadne countered. "In a thousand different ways, a thousand different times from a thousand different people." She snorted. "Even Silenus, as kind as he was, pointed out I didn't belong. Far be it for immortal gods have to witness death up close and personal." She muttered, forgetting her audience, so comfortable in his presence that she began talking freely again.

He reached out and tugged a chunk of her hair free from her sweaty braid. It was entirely silver, almost glowing in the bright sunlight. Dionysus sighed. "I try to forget you are mortal. I don't like to think about it, and what it means."

"Neither do I." Ariadne told him dryly. "But it's rather hard to forget when you're surrounded by people who don't age and laugh frequently at people who do."

"You have been hanging around the wrong people up there, that much is clear." Dionysus grimaced. "Yet another thing I should have helped with." He put both hands on his face and pulled down, lower eyelids stretching downwards. "How am I going to fix this?" He complained dramatically, letting go of his face and flopping over to lie on her again.

Ariadne took a moment to reflect back on her awe and shyness when she had first met Dionysus and how far she had come from there.

She didn't have time to respond to his rhetorical question. Hermes, the god of messengers appeared in a flicker of light, rocking back on his winged sandals.

"Good, good, you're not busy. Nice to see no one got smote. Got kind of worried when I felt that spike of energy earlier." Hermes laughed, and it had a distinct undertone of nervousness that piqued Ariadne's curiosity. What was there for the other gods to fear when the god of wine and parties lost his temper? Sobriety? He certainly wouldn't lose control over his powers. Not after how hard he had worked to get control.

"Dad sent me to check on you." He added, glancing at them and then away like a hummingbird not sure if it should land or not.

"I'm fine." Dionysus's voice from Ariadne's shoulder was both muffled and petulant.

"Yeah?" Hermes sounded wary and not confident. "Then you should probably go see Dad. You worried him when you destroyed your wing of the palace."

# Chapter 9

ARIADNE STIFFENED, shock hitting her like a bucket of cold water. "You did what?" She tried to get her mental sea legs with this new, slightly terrifying information. Dionysus cared about her leaving and perceived rejection enough he had destroyed part of Olympus.

The god tucked into her shoulder like a blanket said nothing, but clung to her tighter. He could destroy buildings on a whim and yet held her like she was the only safe thing in the world. Ariadne decided it wasn't a train of thought that she wanted to go down.

"Right. Of course you did, you silly man. Right." She repeated and sighed from the bottom of her soul. She ignored Hermes's her enormous eyes full of surprise.

"Look, there's no point in going back right now." Seeing as the reasons she left were still valid. Still mortal. "Why don't we go visit that one king, the one with the new hybrid grapes? Give it a while before you head back. Take some time to get your head on straight." It would take him time to adjust to the fact she wouldn't be returning to Olympus with him. She would need time to adjust, too.

Dionysus responded instantly, seeing straight through her hedging. "I'm not going back without you." But he clearly wasn't thinking straight if he thought he could bring a mortal woman with him openly.

Hermes gave Ariadne a sharply speculative look. Ariadne didn't like it, or the trace of amusement she could see under it. She gave Hermes the hairy eyeball for a moment.

"We'll talk about it." She lied, not intending to budge an inch.

"We can go see Demeter and help her can too." Dionysus responded snidely, still clinging to her tightly, smearing lipstick onto her sweaty neck.

She inhaled sharply. They were going to be going below the belt, were they? "Well, if you want to go back to the Underworld to hang out with Persephone and Hades, feel free. I can practice making pickles." She finished ominously, thinking hard about suggestively shaped pickles in his direction.

She could feel him smile into the crook of her neck and flushed, heat creeping up her neck to her ears. When she looked up, Hermes was gone.

———◉———

THEY visited the King Maron, he of the hybrid grapes, although Ariadne knew they would visit Demeter afterwards. If only just to tease her.

The king had started and organized the worship of Dionysus on his small rural island. He had even created some entirely new varieties of wine. They didn't come up to the standard of wine on Olympus, but they were close. Despite this, the man was a priest of Apollo, amusingly enough.

Maron, once he had calmed down about a personal visit from a god, was actually fairly charming. He was also young, handsome and, despite the size and rural nature of his kingdom, fairly rich. He was also single. That turned out to be a problem.

"Would you like to see the vineyards?" Maron offered, eyes flickering to the empty pocket of air beside her where no one stood.

"Sure." Ariadne agreed easily. "He'll be sleeping a while anyway after the party last night. We might as well not wait up." Or let their host work himself into a frothing frenzy of anxiety.

When Dionysus woke, he would do one of two things. He would either find Ariadne like she had a beacon attached or wander around poking his nose into everything, causing chaos as he went.

Dionysus, predictably, found her at the most awkward moment possible. Ariadne walked out of the King's bedroom wearing new clothes with her hair still wet from bathing. Never mind that she had used the communal bath earlier, it looked as if they had just had a casual hookup. His expression didn't even flutter, but Ariadne could feel the sharp edge under the deceptively docile expression.

For the first time since her lover had rescued her off Naxos, she wondered what Dionysus would have done if she had taken other lovers or attempted to. He certainly hadn't seemed pleased at Theseus's attempt to claim her.

"Did I miss something?" Dionysus asked, removing the sleep crumbs out of his eyes with careful, sharp movements to not disturb his makeup.

Maron visibly flushed, unable to look away from the casually half dressed god, painted and pierced.

"I fell into the biggest pile of fertilizer I've ever seen. It was the opposite of dignified." Ariadne told him, tugging on the too long sleeves of her borrowed dress. "His Majesty kindly offered me his wife's old clothes to change into."

"You're married?" Dionysus feigned surprised, hooking his arm around Ariadne's waist and pulling her into him. His fingers rubbed the skin under the hem of her shirt like a worry stone.

Maron looked sad for a moment. "I was. It was an arranged match from when we were children. She was more like my sister, to be honest. So when she wanted out of the match, there were no hard feelings." His expression said that he missed her, but Ariadne wasn't touching that issue with a pole.

Dionysus hummed under his breath. "Well, let's go try some of the wine, if Ariadne's done inspecting the plants." He said brightly and the king foolishly relaxed.

"Of course! I'm honored to share my selection with you." Maron agreed, cheeks glowing. Ariadne had a sudden suspicion why his arranged marriage hadn't worked out.

She didn't trust Dionysus's smile. It was his normal smile, but his eyes were these of a god, not the man she had fallen for.

———◆———

ON their way to the cellar, Dionysus dropped back to ask casually, "So, was he any good?"

Ariadne swatted his side as best she could with him, practically walking in lockstep with her. "Don't be like that. Double standards are ugly."

His expression didn't change. "That good, huh?"

Dionysus was a man, but he was also a god and both were ugly when jealous. Double standards or not, the king might yet have a fate as a smear on the ground if Ariadne didn't do something. Despite the urge to goad her lover slash friend about his hypocrisy, she would do the right thing. Grudgingly.

"He kept asking if everything he did pleased you. The man looked at me and only saw you." She didn't bother to keep the resignation out of her voice. "Maron told me how he had seen you once at one of your festivals as a child and decided to make you the patron god of his entire country."

Dionysus stared straight ahead for a long moment before he sighed. He glanced at her and said, "I overreacted a bit, then."

Ariadne didn't bother answering.

The rest of the evening was pleasant, only noteworthy was the way Maron turned completely red when his patron god drank his wine and complimented it. The flush stayed the rest of the night, going all the way to the tips of his ears every time he took a drink. Dionysus softened enough to admit to her on their way back to their rooms.

"He is rather attractive."

Ariadne felt her mood plummet like Icarus had from the sky. "For you, of course. Who am I compared to a god? Nothing. Not even worth a look." She said bitterly, closing the bedroom door behind them. She ran her hands over her face. "I need to sleep." She decided, but stopped.

Dionysus stood in front of her, arms crossed. "You were right. I do have double standards." He admitted grouchily, flooring her. "Sex is fun, but it's just sex for me. It's not for you." He raised a challenging eyebrow at her. Ariadne looked away and couldn't think of anything to say.

"You get attached." Dionysus told her with a frown.

"Is that supposed to be a bad thing?" Ariadne demanded. "If we're friends, then why is it wrong of me to want a lover as well?"

"I'm right here!" He exclaimed frustratedly, gesturing broadly to himself, glittering green eyes stark against his dark eyeliner. His wrist bangles rattled with the force of the movement.

# Chapter 10

ARIADNE THREW HER HANDS in the air, countering, "You don't think of me as anything but as a friend. You said it yourself. Sex means nothing to you."

"What in the name of Hades gave you the impression I don't think of you as a lover?" Dionysus demanded, affronted, hands on his hips.

Ariadne glared, her frustration boiling over. "The way you never introduced me to anyone as your lover. Then the way you avoided me and even stopped having sex with me. You've never even given me a reason why for any of it." She took a ragged breath, eyes full of tears despite herself. . "Things like that give me the impression you don't think of me as a lover."

She added bitterly, "Or much of me at all."

Dionysus opened his mouth. Closed it. Licked his lips. "Oh."

Ariadne pushed past him, desperate to get some fresh air. On the balcony, the cold air outside stripped the warmth of the room from her in an instant.

The stars glittered in the sky above like a blanket of black velvet with icy white sapphires. Night and darkness obscured the rest of the world like a dream. The stone of the balcony railing dug into her shaking hands, unbending under her franticly spasming hands as she resisted the urge to bury her face in her hands and sob.

It didn't stop the tears. The nighttime chill stole the heat from them before they finished reaching her chin, leaving her face both cold and wet. She breathed carefully through her gritted teeth and let them come, releasing the pain. In, out. In, out. Let the hurt come out through the tears and stop hurting her anymore. Ariadne let it out.

When she was done, empty, tired and numb in more ways than one, she went back in. She didn't see Dionysus in the room. She crawled into the empty bed and pulled the blankets over her.

<hr>

OF course, then Ariadne couldn't actually sleep. It figured. She had bypassed tired and leapt straight into the impossible arena of too tired to sleep. She flipped and flopped like a beached fish.

She got up and went back out to the balcony. The cold was worse now, digging into her bones like it was hungry for her warmth. The stars seemed untouchable and distant. She went back in, shoulders slumped, disappointed and frost in her knotted hair.

The room was still empty.

Suddenly, Ariadne couldn't take it anymore. She left the bedroom, prowling the palace halls just for something to do that wasn't sitting with her thoughts and feelings. It wasn't as interesting as she thought it might have been. But it was something to do.

Ariadne had a pang of sympathy for her mad, twisted twin. He had to have been so bored, trapped in the labyrinth. But then, he ate anyone who might have been able to keep him company.

Suddenly, for the first time, Ariadne wondered why Dionysus was so alone. He was well liked and beloved. What reason did he have to put walls up with people?

Having them with her made sense. Loving a short-lived person was just grief waiting to happen, and immortals didn't handle that kind of thing gracefully. It was a pain they were not equipped to handle and so they avoided it, distancing themselves from the suffering of mortal lives.

The gods were powerful enough the toy with dynasties of mortal royalty on whims, yet they were insecure enough to lash out at any perceived rejection.

Ariadne had too much time to think during her time on Olympus, and most of it wound up being more than vaguely blasphemous and judgmental. Truly, she had stewed on her negative feelings for too long. It had verged on her being poisoned, unknowing. It was one of her many reasons to not return there.

Just before the sun began peeking through the clouds, servants began filtering through the halls. Ariadne returned to her room, not wanting to be underfoot. Or worse, need to explain the reason for her insomnia to their host.

The bedroom was still empty. Her heart fell. Ariadne sighed and got ready for the day, anyway. No matter how much it hurt, she had to keep going.

Maron was polite but visibly disappointed that there was only her at breakfast. She gave him a polite smile and felt small. He gamely offered to show her the rest of the estate despite the lack of divinity accompanying her. Ariadne declined, fists clenched in her lap. They had come for Dionysus to visit the king. If he wasn't around, there wasn't much for Ariadne to do besides take up space.

Her head cleared by the time the midday meal rolled around, and she asked to see how Maron blended his wines. It was a secret process naturally, but being the close companion of the literal god of wine got her a pass.

She learned quickly over the next few days and just as quickly lost patience when Dionysus didn't return or show his face. Ariadne had told him how she felt and he had abandoned her without so much as a goodbye or even telling her he was leaving.

Maron approached her that night before she went to her room. "Are you two having problems?" He asked tentatively, looking like he was regretting opening his mouth.

Ariadne closed her eyes and gritted her teeth. "You could say that." There was no way she could admit that she was hopelessly in love with a god. One that had just realized it would never work between them and cut their losses immediately, without a word.

Maron hesitated. "I'm not an expert in love, but I could lend you an ear. Or shoulder." He added cautiously, watching her blink back frustrated tears. "I have some experience in matters of troubled love." He finished self depreciatingly.

What did she have to lose? She let her hand slip off the doorknob and went with the king to his private study.

Maron sat across from her and admitted bluntly. "My marriage failed because I preferred men to woman and my wife had the opposite problem. Our parents assumed we would be agreeable to, shall we say, cover for each other's issues."

"Let me guess, it didn't work out because having secret affairs on the side doesn't quite cut it for happiness." Ariadne guessed tiredly, gratified by his nod.

"Are you, this is difficult to say," Maron licked his lips. "Are you a secret lover of his?"

She chewed her lip, thinking. "No, but I feel like one. Or did. Pretty sure he's not sure if he wants me as a lover or not." She admitted, feeling wildly vulnerable and regretting every word out of her mouth. What was she doing?

He frowned, got up, and grabbed a book from his shelf. He flipped through it , staring at the page blankly for a moment before closing it. "No one in the mortal realm can agree whether Dionysus is a very old god indeed, or a very young one. But either way, to those who look, it's well known that most of his quests in love have been very brief."

Ariadne gave him the blank stare of incomprehension. "I hardly expected to be an exception."

Maron shook his head. "No, I meant they mostly seem to last a few nights. At most." He met her gaze earnestly. "He may not have the knowledge of how to behave in a relationship, or what a lover might expect of him."

"He's my first relationship as well, but why do I have to do all the emotional labor?" Ariadne retorted, anger flaring up like an ember reigniting under an accelerant.

He closed his mouth. He gave her a sideways look. "Most people would be happy to do whatever it took to please a god."

"My mother was half god. My father was part god. It didn't make them better people, just more careless with others' lives." Ariadne told Maron flatly, deeply unamused at the turn in the conversation.

"Any relationship where one person has all the power or responsibilities is a bad one. If it's not equal, it's just servitude," She thought of some of the stories she had heard over the years, "Or slavery."

"And if he can't give you that?" Maron asked her quietly, and Ariadne had just about enough of this, whatever it was.

"He's a god. The only things they can't do are the ones they don't want to." She told him before getting up from her chair. "Much obliged by the talk and the advice to treat him like an incapable infant, but I don't want children."

Ariadne had stomped back all the way to her still empty rooms before she realized the man she had just spoken to had blue eyes. Maron had brown eyes.

# Chapter 11

THE MAN SHE HAD TALKED to was not the same one she had spoken to at dinner. It wasn't Dionysus in disguise. She could tell that much, but beyond that, she didn't know. Not knowing who was messing with her pissed Ariadne off.

She packed nothing. She had nothing. Just as when she fled Crete, she had nothing but the clothes on her back with her. It was something that made things infinitely easier and more painful. She had nothing. No worldly possessions or lover to hold her close.

Ariadne approached Maron, checked the color of his eyes, and informed him politely she was heading out. He thanked her for her company, like she was someone important. She tried not to laugh at him. She did, however, warn him.

"I'm leaving because I had a truly awful conversation with someone who looked identical to you last night. I was in quite a mood before I remembered you didn't have blue eyes. It would be wise to put the word out you might have a double running around."

Maron swallowed, going pale. "Thank you." He swallowed again, likely thinking of some of the more notorious shapeshifters among the immortals. "I will send you with money and clothes. It would do me a dishonor not to." Even her host had realized Ariadne had no worldly means. Dionysus hadn't even left her a single coin.

Ariadne accepted his offer. While she hated relying on charity, this at least felt like a trade of some dubious sort. "Tell Dionysus, if he comes by and wants to know where I am, that I went to practice my pickling techniques. Then look at his crotch for a moment. He'll understand."

"Understand what?" Maron asked, looking alarmed at her implications.

"That I am furious, but also want him to know where I am so we can talk." She translated for the man who likely feared being turned into a grapevine for offending Dionysus. "If he wants to talk." Ariadne added quietly, already planning on getting passage on a ship headed to the area closest to Demeter's home.

⸻ ◉ ⸻

SHE got kidnapped by pirates.

Pirate raids happened fairly frequently in the region, growing more prominent by the year as more discontented and frequently wronged women joined the crews. The entire ship was captured. The pirates stripped everyone of their belongings, money and, in some cases, clothes if they were fine enough.

Being the gifts of a king, Ariadne's clothes were fine enough for confiscation. Unlike the other near naked nobility and merchants on the deck, she was comfortable in her near nudity. Traveling in a group known for its orgies had strange upsides, as it turned out.

In an odd twist of fate, it is her past as the princess of the Labyrinth that saved her. The first mate, a vaguely familiar young woman, recognized her.

"Princess Ariadne." She said, voice reverent before bowing to Ariadne. The other pirates stop harassing the passengers to stare at them. "I never took the time to thank you for saving everyone."

Ariadne shrugged, the sea wind stinging against her slowly burning skin. "I never took the time to know your name."

"It's Coronis." The young woman told her promptly. "Thank you for saving my brother and I."

Despite his short-sightedness and lechery, Theseus had been the one to end the nightmare of the Minotaur. "Theseus was the real hero." She admitted grudgingly. "I didn't do all that much." Ariadne demurred, guilt over her failed escape attempt eating at her. She had tried to leave the tributes to their gory demise.

Coronis spoke sharply, stalking forward. She got into Ariadne's face aggressively. "You took the time to guide me and my brother through the labyrinth, and comfort him when he wept in fear of the Minotaur. You took the time to ensure our escape, even when you had to navigate the labyrinth alone afterwards. Princess, you are a hero." Coronis dared her to disagree.

The Captain of the now avidly eavesdropping pirates sauntered over. "All that and you still got dumped on an empty island for your trouble by the prince. Rumor is you got picked up by a god afterwards. That true?" She inspected Ariadne, who had sweat now dripping from her skin, despite standing there in nothing but her underwear.

"Yeah." Ariadne shrugged, sun burned skin tight on her shoulders. "How'd that come out?" She risked asking, taking a deep breath from her too small lungs.

Coronis told her dryly, "When the families of the tributes sent a search party back for you, the island was empty. There was, however, a massive grove of grapevines and ivy in the middle of the beach." She smirked, adding, "One sailor was stupid enough to eat some grapes and was drunk for three days."

"Subtle, Dionysus is not." Ariadne agreed with a groan, rubbing the heel of her palm into her eye, where a headache promised to bloom. Darkness flirted at the edge of her vision.

"Theseus's face when he heard the god of orgies picked you up was hilarious." Coronis revealed with vicious amusement, ushering her to the shade to sit down with a nod at the Captain. "Where should we be letting you off at then, Princess? Seeing as I owe you a debt and the crew doesn't want to anger your lover."

Ariadne went to answer, but the world went dark as she finally succumbed to heatstroke.

———◦———

SHE woke up back in her cabin with cold packs on her pulse points, still wearing only her underwear. Hermes sat in the chair that didn't exist before, flipping a familiar ball of string back and forth between his hands. The last she had seen of it, Theseus had it as they fled the Labyrinth.

"Can I help you?" She offered, as the god of thieves snatched the ball out of the air, clearly having been deep in thought.

"That's what I'm here for, actually. To help you, not the other way around." He told her cheerfully, in such a way that Ariadne instinctively knew his mood was fake.

"Why would you do that?" She questioned, a cold pack sliding off her neck.

Hermes smiled wider. It looked painful. "Why wouldn't I want to help out my baby brother's lover?"

"You got ordered to, huh?" She placed a cold pack on her face before realizing it was warm. She took them all off and sat up on the bed to face the god across from her.

"Is it that obvious?" He grimaced, bouncing the thread ball one handed.

"Where is Dionysus? What's his problem with me?" She asked, knowing she was talking to the god of liars and despite that, he was still her best bet at a straight answer. Her life had definitely taken a few weird turns lately.

He gave her a bewildered look. "I have no idea what has happened with this situation aside from turning into a clusterfuck."

"I had a fight with Dionysus. He didn't come back. Someone pretended to be my host and gave me bad relationship advice. I left before Dionysus's new favorite vintner got creamed on the sidelines." Ariadne summed up. "Your turn. What's going on with Dionysus?"

Hermes looked thoughtful. "That makes sense." He drummed his fingers on his thigh before snapping them. "Right. Still have no idea." He gave her a charming grin, as if he thought that would get him out of answering.

Ariadne got off the bed, staggered, caught her balance, and then sat in his lap. The grin fell off his face. She looked up at him, slightly startled at the height difference even sitting down. "Right. I'll ask one. more. time." She laced her arms around his neck and pulled her face next to his ear to hiss. "What is going on?"

She could see his throat move as he swallowed. "You are a surprisingly scary woman." Hermes shifted like he wanted to fidget and realized what it did with her in his lap.

"As far as I can tell, my brother doesn't know how to use his words and express how he feels about you." Ariadne's breath stilled in her lungs. How he felt- could it be? Hermes continued on like he hadn't felt her tense up, despite the flickering look at her and away.

"Dionysus's either sulking or pestering people for advice and ignoring all of it and beginning to panic the longer it goes on. The body double was probably Dad. He's the worst. At romantic advice." He tacked on distractedly.

Ariadne wrinkled her nose. "I am so glad he didn't hit on me. Would have broken character, I suppose."

"It's uh, actually really strange he didn't, but meeting you, I think I'm starting to understand why. Dionysus likes dangerous women." Hermes sighed. "Dad does not." He added, trying to peel her hands off him. She obligingly let him think he could have his freedom when he wanted it.

"You seem like an intelligent person who actually knows the person I'm having trouble with." She said, instead of asking if Dionysus was in love with her like she wanted to.

"I dislike the sound of this." Hermes picked her up bodily and sat her back on the bed, sitting down and jiggling his leg in a blur.

# Chapter 12

ARIADNE IGNORED THAT. "Do you have any advice?"

"Alright, that's fair." He admitted, running both hands through his mop of curls. "Right. Dionysus isn't spontaneously going to learn how to use words for his feelings. That's going to be a long-term thing. The problem is, if he can't put how he feels into words, he doesn't know what to do."

Ariadne nods and catches the ball of string thrown at her. "So, what, a question-and-answer session where we stab around in the dark?" She throws the ball back at him, surprised how easily he snatched it out of the air to juggle it again.

"No, that would require words. The solution here is going to have to leave words out of it." Hermes lobbed the ball back to her.

Ariadne bounced the ball of string in her palm and had to snatch it before it got away from her. It didn't help her think, so she tossed it back to him. "What are you suggesting?"

"Sex." Hermes tossed the ball back. She barely caught it with the tips of her nails.

"Be more specific." Ariadne ordered, throwing it back and hitting his chest with it.

"Talk during sex. Doing something else might help him think." He threw the ball to her. "Or not think enough to let the words come out. Whichever."

Ariadne re-rolled the ball of thread where it had come undone, thinking about it. "I have been told by multiple older women the fastest way to get a man to dump me is to talk about feelings. Specifically, his feelings. You're suggesting I murder what's left of my relationship in the hope of understanding it. A relationship that apparently even the gods can't quite wrap their minds around."

"Pretty much." He agreed, watching her fingers move the thread, round and round as she reformed the ball.

"Why would I want to do that?" She asked, more to herself than Hermes. "Ruin the last good thing I have left in my life." Ariadne muttered, sighed and tossed the completed ball back at him.

He caught it without looking at it. "Do you want to be immortal?" He asked bluntly, startling her. Was he implying...?

"For its own sake? No." She smiled thinly at his surprised look. "I've seen what immortality does to you gods. It's a miserable existence if you're not careful, and there is never, ever an end in sight. Even the Titans still suffer in the depths of Tartarus, no end to be had, no relief for the rest of eternity."

She continued, "At least as a mortal I can escape the pain and unjust rulers to the Underworld and the relief of the waters of Lethe. You have no such option, mostly." She felt her smile crumble and looked away, and caught sight of her clothes folded at the foot of her bunk.

Hermes was completely, unnaturally still, considering her with a slightly tilted head. "You might not want to be immortal, but I think you would handle it well." He said thoughtfully. Then there was the full weight of a god wrapped in the shape of a mortal scrutinizing her. The air grew heavy and hard to breathe. It felt like her skin was no protection from being seen.

"You would do well to take him up on it when Dionysus offers it, lest you break my brother's heart forever." His expression grew cruel, matching the intensity of the pressure still slowly building. "As you just said yourself, immortals have no escape. He would grieve you forever."

Ariadne rolled her eyes, ignoring his show of power through force of will and knowledge he genuinely cared for Dionysus. "I thought you were supposed to be a good liar. No emotion, no matter how intense, lasts forever. Not even for gods."

The pressure broke like mist before the sun. "You're no fun. Why can't you be a romantic?" He sulked for a moment before he added knowingly. "I know you love him."

"I'm a romantic." She defended. "I'm also terrified of falling in love and expecting things I will never get and be perpetually heartbroken over it. My mother loved my father that way. It's an ugly, painful way to live." Ariadne suddenly understood why Hermes was a dangerous god. He was too damn friendly and likable. She had never talked openly like this to someone else except Dionysus.

She was abruptly, sharply aware of how lonely her existence was.

"So tell him what you want." Hermes threw the ball back at her.

"What if I get it? What if it makes him unhappy, and he does it anyway?" She threw the ball back harder than necessary. She thought briefly of what Hermes implied she could have before recoiling from the thought. Some temptations were too much to resist.

"Isn't that what you're doing to yourself?" He tossed the ball back and forth between his hands, gaining speed until there was only a blurred red arc between them. "You two really are a pair." Hermes sighed, sounding put upon and once more completely fake.

"I don't know what else to do." Ariadne said, reaching for her clothes at the foot of the bed and wiggling into her dress with a hiss of pain. The fabric rasped against her angry sunburn like a wire brush. She stood, straightening out the material of her dress.

She caught the ball by reflex, not really aware of it until it's in her hand, warm in a way thread shouldn't be. It also hadn't snapped or frayed once in the rough walled labyrinth. That was odd, it had been ordinary if high-quality thread when she had bought it.

"You ready to head out to Demeter's and get your canning on?" He changed the subject, surveying her newly clothed state with unconcealed relief.

Ariadne tried to swallow back the whine that wanted to come out of her. She managed not to grimace. "If he doesn't come to talk soon, I'm leaving with Persephone." She threatened mournfully before belatedly realizing the deeper connotations her threat had.

Hermes, the bastard, just laughed at her and offered Ariadne his hand. She took the provided hand and the world blurred around her, ground vanishing under her feet.

———◦———

ARIADNE stumbled, overwhelmed with vertigo. They were down the road from where Demeter lived. The world lost clarity, suddenly blurry as the reflection of smoke in a grease smeared mirror. After a moment, all the strange effects of travel vanished. Except the nausea.

Hermes laughed at her again when she threw up after their arrival. Ariadne resented that she quite liked him. "Are you sure you're not pregnant, hmm?" He said laughing, walking backwards while facing her on the path to Demeter and Persephone's home.

Ariadne gave him the look that deserved. "Even you're not that fast."

His face creased with horror. "Not me! I meant my brother's spawn."

She cackled at his nervous discomfort. "As if I let anyone between my legs without making sure that's not a problem. No, Asclepius was quite helpful in that regard." She concluded with a nod, grateful for the birth control.

"Would having my brother's children be so bad?" Hermes frowned at her.

Ariadne sighed heavily. Men. "First of all, you're not the one squeezing a babe the size of a watermelon out of your genitals. Second, no children are better than unwanted children." She paused to see if any of this had sunk in. He was grimacing but nodding. Ah, Ariadne was growing fond of him. So many positive signs of the ability to learn.

She stopped walking. He stopped as well, rocking back on his heels. "Third, my twin was the Minotaur."

# Chapter 13

"I HAVE THE SAME BLOOD in my veins as him. I don't know what that would do to any child I have. A child with the long lifespan of a demigod and the pain of being outcast? A child that is a monster, hungry for human flesh and near unkillable? I don't want to bring either of those things into the world, or any variation possible."

"You've had this conversation before, huh," Hermes concluded when they began walking again.

"Dionysus never asked if I wanted kids." Ariadne admitted, wanting to gloss over it.

Hermes gave her a soft look, as if he could see her insecurities. "He's probably thought about what might happen to his children as well. His childhood was...not the best."

Demeter puts a hand on his shoulder, stopping him from walking into her. "That's the understatement of the century. Hello, Ariadne." She smiled at Ariadne with too many teeth. The goddess could never seem to remember how many mortals had. Forty? Fifty? Something like that.

"I'm surprised you use my name. I expected to be referred to as what I am to you. Canning slave." She returned dryly and was rewarded with Demeter smiling with, oh, that hurt her brain, even more teeth.

"That can be arranged." Demeter agreed.

"Please don't. Dionysus has been in a weird mood lately." Hermes said slightly desperately, "You know how he can get." He added with a sideways look and hand gesture.

Demeter sobered up, seeming to catch the unmentioned reference. "I see. You can tell me more about it inside. We're due for rain soon." She added with a glare upwards.

———◆———

PERSEPHONE cut Ariadne's threatened escape attempt short by being at Olympus saying her yearly farewells. Demeter, as it turned out, was also on her way to Olympus. She hadn't been expecting any visitors.

"It's not as if I received any notice about it beforehand." Demeter said reprovingly, over the rim of her wine cup.

Ariadne winced. "I'm sorry. I can stay somewhere else."

Demeter waved her off. "It's not that I mind you being here, so much as I would have preferred to be here as a host. My business on Olympus is, unfortunately, business and I cannot avoid it. I need to talk to Zeus about his so-called rainstorms."

She smirked at Ariadne, suddenly amused. "I'm afraid I'm going to have to leave you here alone with the spiders."

Ariadne cringed and took a gulp of Demeter's Olympian wine. "I understand. Thank you for letting me stay here."

Demeter rolled her eyes. "Just invite me to the wedding when you two get your shit together."

Hermes came back into the room from a suspiciously long bathroom break, smiling like a satisfied canary. "I wouldn't bet on that being for a while. They both have commitment issues." He confided in the older goddess, taking a seat next to Ariadne.

"How many kids versus wives do you have again?" Ariadne asked pointedly, pouring herself another cup of wine.

Demeter cackled, kicking her bare feet up on the table. "Nothing wrong with a few babies on the wrong side of the blanket."

"Sure." Ariadne agreed, feeling mellow as the wine started to hit. She poured Hermes a drink, handing it over without further comment.

She felt bad for the messenger god, honestly. He was overworked and frequently drawn into the weird shit other gods generated. Being a parent on top of all that with way, way too many kids had to be anxiety inducing.

He took the offered cup, drinking deeply before asking, "How do you not have a higher tolerance for drink?"

"How would I get Olympian wine?" Ariadne questioned, blinking slowly. "I have a good tolerance for mortal wine. Good enough, at any rate."

Hermes set his cup down. "You are practically attached at the hip to the god of wine." He emphasized with both hands, eyebrows crunched together.

She grinned at him, putting her chin on her hand. "He is. That means he likes all wine, not just the stuff on Olympus." Ariadne caught herself having the urge to giggle and fought it down.

Demeter looked up, then frowned into her cup. "I need to get going." She stood, patted Hermes on the head, patted Ariadne the same way, and left.

Ariadne resisted the urge to have more of the wine. She suspected getting drunk around Hermes would lead to committing some kind of crime. Or she'd open her mouth again and horrify him some more. It was a fifty/fifty chance.

"Why do you look nervous?" She tilted the wine in her cup idly.

"You're not going to hit on me, are you?" He looked at her from the corner of his narrowed eyes.

Ariadne snickered. "You realize I was threatening you earlier, right? I was planning on biting off your ear if you gave me shit, not reach for your dick."

"That is both comforting and deeply disturbing." Hermes seemed to cheer up despite his nervous words. He paused, his drink almost to his mouth. "My ear though?"

She smiled at him knowingly. "Ears are sensitive without being life threatening. A pretty, mostly naked woman climbs into a man's lap and gets close to his face. He's not thinking about her teeth going through his ear. Doesn't even cross his mind." She set the wine cup down, putting temptation further away.

Hermes still hadn't taken a drink, staring at her. He sets his drink down. "Right. Time for me to go wash my socks. Gotta go. Nice talking to you. I think."

Ariadne waved one hand, and he was gone before her hand finished the first motion. "What was that about? He wears sandals." She asked the empty room, not expecting an answer.

Dionysus sank into Hermes's vacated chair, likely still warm. "He's realizing he misjudged a situation badly." He explained, dragging the abandoned cup of wine toward him and drinking it in one smooth gesture.

"What, he really thought I was hitting on him?" She let the giggle out now, relaxing at the presence of Dionysus. She could smell flowers drifting from his floral wreathed crown.

He gave her a conspiratorial grin. "Hermes definitely thought you were hitting on him. He was probably nervous because I told him if he hit on you, I'd pull off his wings. And then he learned he should have been nervous, but for a very different reason." He poured himself another cup of wine, still smiling.

"You surround yourself with women famous for ripping people apart and thought you would date a meek woman?" Ariadne let the judgement creep into her voice. She deliberately didn't address the conversational elephant in the room.

Dionysus shrugged, turning to put his feet on her lap. "I've never actually had more than a week long sex marathon relationship, so he was probably just going off his preferences towards girls with a secret kinky side." Ariadne peeled his sandals off and dropped them to the floor. His dark violet toenail polish gleamed with perfection in the dim kitchen light.

With a hand around his ankle, she asked at last, "Are you ready to talk now?"

"I am." Dionysus confirmed, wiggling his pretty purple toes at her. "Originally, I was going to have Hermes bring you back to Olympus to talk, but he pointed out Demeter's place was closer to neutral ground. It worked out that Demeter was planning on harassing Zeus about the rain for some crop related reason anyway, so it's just us."

Ariadne hummed, falling silent, suddenly not sure what to say. He wiggled his feet in her lap. She traced the inside curve of his foot with a fingernail, hand tightening on his ankle when he tried to pull it away.

"No, stop, it tickles." He tugged gently at his foot, grinning at her. Obligingly, she stopped and let his foot go.

"Why did you stop?" Dionysus pouted, feet not moving from her lap.

"You asked me to." She told him cheerily, grinning at his huff. He sprawled backwards in his chair.

"I thought about what you said to me." He said quietly.

# Chapter 14

ARIADNE KNEW IMMEDIATELY he was referring to her list of complaints. She was also a bit too tipsy to safely get into the conversation, but didn't want to put it off any longer either.

"I'm sorry. I didn't know that was how it felt for you, but I should have thought about it." He sighed, arms flopping over the side of the chair to dangle limply. "I was trying to think of ways to do better when Hermes pointed out leaving in the middle of the argument and not coming back was..." He searched for a word and winced as he said it, "Cruel."

Ariadne liked this apology. She clearly owed Hermes something nice. "Hermes apparently gives good advice. He's right. Every time we ran into trouble, you run away and leave me alone. I don't know what you want with me, Dionysus." She sat his feet gently on the ground.

"I was your lover and then you don't want me anymore physically. You brought your mother back and-" She hesitated, voice catching.

"And I spent less time with you, leaving you questioning why you're hiding your identity for a man who doesn't want you." Dionysus filled in, staring at his bare feet on the floor.

"We'll always be friends. I would never abandon our friendship." She reassured him quietly, stomach churning.

His head snapped up. "I don't want to be your friend." He spat out.

Ariadne recoiled, mouth dropping open in shock.

"What I want," He gritted out, poisonous green eyes glittering unnaturally bright, "Is for you to hold me tightly at night, to look at me and see through my shit and love me, anyway. The way you always do."

Ariadne opened her mouth, but Dionysus continued, seeming to build momentum. "I want you by my side, and not disguised. Not just my friend. As my partner. As my wife. " He finished softly, searching her face. "I love you Ariadne." He breathed.

Ariadne met him halfway for a brief kiss. She pulled back, feeling like she could float away.

Reality hit and the euphoria turned to dread. He loved her. Her mortality couldn't make it anything besides a tragedy in the making.

"I love you too." She tried to show how sincere she was, that it wasn't an automatic, trite thing. His expression closed off.

"But what?" He asked, folding his arms and holding his elbows defensively.

"But I can't- I'm not-" She sighed and just said it. "I'm going to die one day. Maybe not today or tomorrow, but one day I will. You won't. I can't break your heart."

Dionysus looked away. "I know that." His fingers tightened on his arms until the skin bulged around his fingers. "I know that." He repeated quietly.

Ariadne stared at her lap, lost and not sure where to go from there. He already loved her. She loved him. Maybe...maybe he could visit her yearly in the Underworld, like Persephone did her husband, Hades.

"But you don't have to."

She looked up. He was staring at a spot over her head, shoulders tight.

"What?" She blurted.

He dropped his gaze to meet hers. "I could have my father make you immortal."

"Why would he agree to that?" Ariadne stood, suddenly unable to stay sitting and almost knocked over her wineglass when she swayed. Dionysus reached out, steading her with gentle vines of ivy and grape. The heavy lassitude of wine vanished.

He said nothing, looking up at her through his thick eyelashes. She swallowed, the tightness in her throat making it uncomfortable. "Your mother died because of him. He owed you both. I'm-" She stopped, not sure what to say. "I'm not someone he would care about enough to go back on his own rules." She finished lamely.

Dionysus got up from his seat and pulled her into his arms, vines twining around them both affectionately. "He would if we were married." Dionysus murmured into her ear. He pulled back with a familiar wicked gleam in his eye, adding, "Especially if the alternative is eternal sobriety."

Ariadne blinked rapidly. He was serious. "Marry?" Weakly, "Me?" She dragged in a lungful of air. Then, not having enough air, she took another shallow breath. The tight bands around her chest seemed to tighten instead of loosening. Another breath. Another. Her available air seemed to get less and less with every breath, leaving her gasping like a fish on dry land.

Dionysus tucked her into his arms and hooked his chin over her shoulder. "Breathe with me. Don't worry, okay? Just breathe with me."

He wasn't the one being offered- no, don't think about it, Ariadne told herself fiercely. She focused on breathing with him and moving past her panic attack. Breathing. In. Out. In. Out.

She felt his chest rise and fall. She focused on the way she remembered it felt under her hands, or the memory of using it as a pillow and falling asleep to the thudding of his strangely slow heartbeat.

Eventually, Ariadne pulled back and buried her face in her hands. "Why would you offer me that?" She asked neutrally as she could, emotional exhaustion dragging her voice into roughness. It wasn't like he didn't have other options, after all.

"Because I love you. Because you deserve more than handing your identity as Ampelos. I don't want you to pretend to be a servant. I want you as yourself, as my equal." Dionysus paused. "Because I realized these past days what it would feel like to live without you. I hate it." He finished venomously, the shape of his pupils slitted like a snake's.

Ariadne put her hands over her mouth and tried to think. "What if I screw it up?" Her eyes burned with tears, throat closing up rapidly, "What if I-"

Dionysus pulled her hands away and held them in his, kissing her knuckles. "I," He reminded her pointedly, "Have screwed up quite a bit in my life. Even if you do, it won't kill you." He emphasized with a careful squeeze.

"Take your time to decide what you want and I'll give it to you," Dionysus promised softly, pulling her back into a tight hug. He pressed a kiss to her shoulder, fingers trailing gently through the silver streak in her hair.

He added, soft enough it was almost inaudible, "But not too much time."

Suddenly, Ariadne knew what the next step was. "They say that drinking wine is to bring the god of wine into your body." She reached out and brought her wineglass between them and took a deliberate sip, maintaining eye contact.

The smile that bloomed across Dionysus's face was part smoldering heat and part delight. "Well, how am I to refuse such an offering?"

— ◆ —

ARIADNE woke up to the sound of broken sobs. She peeled her eyes open and located Dionysus curled up half on her naked stomach.

"What's wrong?" She rasped.

The crying stopped. Dionysus lifted his head to peer through his tangled mess of hair. "Ariadne?" His voice was even hoarser than hers was.

Ariadne blinked and lifted her head further to peer around the room. The room came into focus after a few more seconds of blinking. Vines as thick as her waist crawled throughout the room, heavy with green grapes. Their bedding was on the floor in a heap.

Dionysus himself was naked, covered in bite marks and bruises. From what she briefly saw of his back, deep scratches. Dried fluids liberally streaked the sheets, interspersed with still wet blood smears.

"Are you okay?" She sat up abruptly, dragging him close to inspect his wounds. "What happened?"

He just shook his head, pulled her close and breathed unsteadily into her naked shoulder, tears hot on her skin. Obligingly, Ariadne held him close, terrified by the scene in front of her.

Or she tried to. His back was a mass of ichor filled cuts and what could only be called gouges. There was nowhere safe to touch without hurting him. "I can't remember what happened. Did I... did I hurt you?" She asked, voice cracking and hands shaking as she gingerly rested them on the back of his arms.

"Did you hurt me?" Dionysus laughed, short and bitterly. Ariadne's heart dropped to the floor. He pulled out of the hug to look at her, expression softening. "Of course not. I, on the other hand, am a fucking idiot." He traced her shoulder like it was the softest of silks instead of sticky with blood.

Ariadne belatedly realized she was also covered in bruises and scratches. It just wasn't immediately obvious because none of it hurt and the distraction of the clinging god.

"I'll be the judge of that." She told him firmly. "Tell me what happened."

Dionysus wiped his eyes, smearing blood and eyeliner across his face and reached a hand out, touching her forehead. The alcohol clouded memories of the night before dissolved into crystal clear recall.

They had gone back to her room and had sex, more wine, competitive ranked sex that had led to more wine and then... "We brought your god powers into the bedroom." Ariadne groaned. "We're both idiots." She pressed her head against his, foreheads touching. "But why would you think I died?"

"Because after you passed out, I did too. When I woke up, it was to both of us bleeding everywhere. I'm immortal, it didn't matter to me, but you almost died. All because I wanted to show off and give you on unforgettable night to apologize for being a thoughtless ass."

Dionysus took a deep breath, "But all I did was hurt you again. It feels like all I ever do." He buried his face into her shoulder once more and began to cry again. "I'm sorry."

"I'm sorry too. I agreed to it, despite knowing better..." Ariadne stroked his hair and stared up at the ceiling, crowded with rustling leafy vines. "It was impressive, though." She tried to console him, the memory warming her sore body.

"Yeah?" He didn't lift his head, clinging to her front like a burr.

Ariadne shifted to curl an arm around him and squeeze, suppressing a wince at the movement. "We can't take it back, so might as well own what happened. So yes, it was worth it. Maybe less wine next time."

He stiffened in her arms and pulled back to give her an outraged look. "Next time? There's not going to be a next time! You almost died." His voice cracked, mirroring his fragile expression.

"Because we were both shitfaced." Ariadne pointed out reasonably.

"I thought you were dead." Dionysus told her, voice thick and red-rimmed eyes heavy with more tears. "I thought that using my powers as a god had been too much for you and I thought you were dead." He repeated, shuddering.

# Chapter 15

"I THOUGHT I'D TURNED into my father in the worst way possible, killing the woman I love through stupidity and ego."

"You're definitely not your father. I'm not dead." She assured Dionysus softly, holding both his wet cheeks in her hands. "It's fine. We had fun, but it got out of hand. We both learned a lesson." She summed up gently.

When he just stared at her, dazed, she pulled him in for a rib creaking hug. That seemed to trigger something in him, and he squeezed her back even tighter. They held each other for a long moment before pulling back, cuts beginning to ooze again.

"Let's get cleaned up." Dionysus pulled her to her feet and they stagger to the bathroom. They washed the blood, ichor and remains of far too much sex off each other's skin. Together, they got dressed and began tending to their wounds.

He ran hands heavy with magic over every gouge and tooth mark on her with a frown, her skin tightening as it knitted together under his touch. The remaining cuts looked like something a human would do in a moment of intense passion rather than an animal mauling. The bite marks refuse to heal much at all, bruising spectacularly. Ariadne dug up a bruise balm that she rubbed on them both, not finding a lot of places that didn't need the balm.

"Why can you only heal it a little?" She asked, gently daubing a different paste on his cuts.

"Because I'm trying to be gentle. Even healing magic can destroy if you use too much of it. I won't risk you." Dionysus pressed a kiss to her last scratch, eyelashes tickling the underside of her knee.

"Then there is no reason you can't heal yourself."

"A little pain won't hurt me." He put her leg down and gestured, pulling a stack of clothes out of the air in another absentminded show of power.

"Dionysus." He raised a belligerent eyebrow at her tone and hands her half the stack of clothes.

Ariadne sat it in her lap and lifted her chin. "I don't want you to punish yourself. We are both consenting adults. Bringing your powers into things wasn't the smartest thing we could have done but-"

"I almost lost you!" Dionysus jerked to his feet, snarling inhuman and deep from his chest. "How do you not understand that? Can you not understand what that felt like for me?"

Ariadne bit her lip, but didn't look away. "I've almost died before-" She started, but he cut her off again.

"I didn't love you then!" Dionysus stopped. His hand went to his mouth, touching it gingerly, as if he couldn't believe what had come out of it. He elaborated awkwardly, "I cared you were mine, but the way I feel about you now is different. Losing you then would have been infuriating. Losing you now... I can't. I can't do that." He finished in a whisper, green eyes glossy.

"I told you I wouldn't let anything happen to you. Then I almost killed you right after, with the powers I swore to get under control." He buried his face in his hands. "I always wind up killing anyone who cares about me. I drove two of my aunts and an uncle mad and to their death. My cousins, my nannies, all of them." Dionysus confessed.

"That's a lot of family." Ariadne said numbly.

"All of them are dead now because of me. Sometimes I wonder if my mother asking father to see his true god form was because of me as well." Dionysus took a breath and held it, trying to control his ragged breathing. He begged, "Please don't leave me."

"I won't." Ariadne reassured him. "You didn't lose control last night, remember? We just went further than what I could handle." She acknowledged with a wince.

Dionysus searched her face, looking for something he could understand. "Why aren't you running for the hills?"

"I'm not capable of understanding Olympian tongue, remember? People talked in from of me. I've known about your childhood since the first week on the mountain." Ariadne told him bluntly. "Nothing detailed, just the shape of things." She added at his look of horror.

"I know what I am getting into." She stepped into his personal space, looking at him down then up, meeting his gave steadily. "I want you. I want this."

He kissed her.

There was a knock at the bedroom door.

# Chapter 16

"ARIADNE? MOTHER SENT me to check on you." Persephone's voice came through the closed door, sounding deeply awkward. "I'll-" She stopped talking abruptly, and the door opened.

Dionysus was already up and halfway to the door, but the goddess of the Underworld had already come in with a deeply concerned expression that was rapidly turning horrified at the wreckage of the room.

"Did you kill her?" She asked Dionysus incredulously before seeming to fall into speechlessness.

Ariadne crept out from behind Dionysus. "No, no, I'm fine." She gave Persephone a tremulous smile. "This looks bad, but we were actually getting on really well last night."

Persephone shot her a look. "You've been damn close to dying within the last few hours. I'm the Queen of the Underworld, I can tell." She glanced around the room at the shredded bedding and blackened blood and metallic gold ichor. "Not that the evidence doesn't speak for itself."

"We just got carried away." She wouldn't have bothered defending what she and her lover did in the bedroom, but Dionysus seemed crushed at Persephone's lowered opinion.

"Doing what exactly? Beating the shit out of each other?" Persephone ran a hand through her hair in a gesture remarkably similar to Dionysus and then held it in front of her like it had answers.

"I used my powers." Dionysus admitted, looking at Ariadne with a guilty expression.

Persephone seemed lost. "You got both of you drunk?" Something crossed her face like a shadow. "No, you couldn't have brought madness into the bedroom." She almost seemed to beg.

Ariadne wrinkled her nose. "I didn't even think of it like that." She admitted.

Dionysus gave an uncomfortable shrug. "It was an extension of the religious ecstasy and such."

"Religious ecstasy." Persephone repeated, closing her eyes. "And what is more religious or ecstasy inducing than having sex with a god? Of course."

"He's also the god of a few other related things." Ariadne didn't clarify, but waited for Persephone to make the connections herself. When she gave a faint grimace, Ariadne knew she had come to the right conclusions.

Being a god of erections made for divine stamina and recovery periods unseen outside other fertility deities. Being the god of intoxication and religious frenzied ecstasy and bringing the combination into the bedroom... Ariadne had enjoyed her near death experience immensely. Until her near death experience, so had Dionysus.

Persephone opened her eyes to give Dionysus the most judgmental look she had seen. "I thought better of you." She sounded disappointed.

Dionysus didn't even defend himself, hunching inwards.

"I'm not dead." Ariadne pointed out, irritated.

"You are very lucky to have survived that." Persephone rolled her eyes at Ariadne's mulish shrug. "You're both idiots. I'll be in the kitchen pouring all of Mother's alcohol out." She grumbled, stomping out of the room, muttering something under her breath that sounded like complaints.

Ariadne heaved a sigh, glancing at a downcast Dionysus. She struggled to think of something to say, but nothing came to mind.

ARIADNE emerged from the guest bedroom holding Dionysus's hand, chin thrust up defiantly.

Persephone handed them each a flower crown. Letting go of Dionysus's hand, Ariadne examined the gift. It was a tightly woven crown of blooming, fragrant roses bordered by laurel leaves. It was an exact match for Dionysus's except for the color of the roses.

"What is this?" He asked, glancing from his flower crown to Ariadne's. "Only gods wear laurel leaves, Persephone."

Persephone gestured for them to follow her and walked out of the house to her waiting chariot. It gleamed, the dark yellow of pure gold, a sharp contrast to the pitch black horses harnessed to it. She gathered the reigns in one hand before turning to address them, expression grave. "I know what you asked Zeus for. All of Olympus probably knows by now."

"Father agreed to my request." Dionysus reached over and squeezed Ariadne's hand. "He had no problem with making Ariadne immortal."

Persephone shook her head. "But he doesn't approve, little one. Like he didn't approve of Endymion or of Tithonus. He doesn't like mortals on Olympus or even former mortals."

"Who?" Dionysus is frowning, but Ariadne's heart raced at the names of her two great aunt's formerly mortal lovers.

She explained, "Zeus granted Tithonus immortality but not eternal youth. He also granted Endymion immortality and eternal youth, but left him in an eternal sleep." Ariadne unclenched her fingers from where she had crushed her wreath in her free hand, scattering the petals in the morning breeze.

Dionysus inhaled sharply. Persephone nodded. "I am fond of you Dionysus and proud of the way you took responsibility for yourself by working to control your powers with Mother's help. You are a kind, gentle man and that means more than what you can imagine to me. I would hate to see your happiness and stability destroyed by Zeus's pride."

"So. I will make you and your future bride an offer." Ariadne started at the title, thrilled that it referred to her.

"Come with me to the Underworld this year and show me your love for each other. At the end of winter, I'll offer to turn Ariadne into a goddess as a wedding present. Zeus won't want to be upstaged, and he'll do it himself." Persephone finished her offer and explanation, stepping into her waiting chariot with the grace of the Queen she was.

Ariadne had only half a moment to process the shock of the offer before Dionysus was dragging her onboard the chariot.

"Don't I get as say in this?" She demanded crankily, but didn't let go of his hand.

His smile was huge. "What, you don't want to go?"

# Chapter 17

ARIADNE WAS SO BUSY chewing over the deal that was struck that she barely noticed their arrival into the Underworld. They landed silently in the courtyard of a castle that was mostly concealed in gloom.

There was no visible source of light besides the occasional glowing fungus trailing beside a walking path. Yet everything was dimly visible after a moment of letting Ariadne's eyes adjust. In was a twilight wonderland of shadows. As Ariadne looked, sources of light appeared. Candles in windows, strange phosphorus blue glows in the distance and the intense white of stars. Frogs warbled unseen, hunting the occasional cricket chirp.

"It's so restful." Ariadne relaxed with a sigh. Dionysus was already bounding off the chariot to hug a surprised Hades.

Persephone turned to her and stopped. "Your eyes…"

"Oh, right. I forget about them most of the time." Ariadne touched a spot under her eyes. "Helios is my maternal grandfather. My eyes change color occasionally, but that seems to be it for inheritance." She had attempted to set people on fire with her mind as a child, but had no such luck. Disappointing.

"You forgot about them." Persephone repeated, holding a hand out to steady Ariadne as she stepped out of the chariot. "Your glowing eyes that emit light in the dark."

"It's not like I can see them." Ariadne pointed out reasonably. "Normally they don't glow or anything either." She paused. "Just in the labyrinth, really." Come to think of it, that had probably been eerie for the last set of tributes.

Persephone looked far too intrigued. "I should visit that place one day."

Ariadne almost didn't want to ask, but the sudden fear of waking up with her dead twin standing at the foot of her bed pushed her into it. "Is my brother..." She starts but does not know what she is actually asking.

Persephone seemed to understand her mostly unspoken question. She patted Ariadne on the head. "I keep the Minotaur far from here. His power when alive was tremendous, but he is exceedingly dead. I am the co-ruler of this realm. You have nothing to fear from him."

Ariadne went almost boneless with relief. Then guilt set in. "He's my twin, but I just never could escape the sensation he hated me and wanted me dead." She admitted with a wince as they approached a smiling Hades and cheerily chattering Dionysus.

"He's your what?" Persephone looked at her like she had fallen off the chariot and taken head damage. The other two stilled their conversation to blatantly eavesdrop together.

"My twin. Shared a womb for a while." Ariadne repeated. "What's so strange about that?"

Persephone looked at her husband, who looked politely baffled at whatever question she was asking with her eyes. She turned back to Ariadne. "Do you even have any mortal human in you?"

"Not currently." She said reflexively, then hid her face in her hands and hissed at a snickering Dionysus through her fingers, "You are such a bad influence."

Persephone either didn't get the joke or blessedly faked ignorance and apathy. "I really need to get a look at that labyrinth and that cursed bull. Demigod or not, Pasiphaë shouldn't have been able to conceive a normal child from the bull."

"Well, I've always theorized he sucked all the magic up in the womb. All the other women in my family are terrifying witches." Ariadne suggested, unable to hide her jealousy. "All I got was an evil twin."

"Yes, but since you're a bastard, we're not actually related, distantly or otherwise." Dionysus said with a lascivious waggle of his eyebrows that made her giggle.

"No. Absolutely not." Persephone said, dropping a hand on Ariadne. A strange sensation like viscous water settled over her and then was gone.

Hades looked at Dionysus. "What precisely happened to have my wife drag both of you here for supervision? As well as put your lover under a chastity spell?"

Dionysus looked mutinous, glaring at what Ariadne could only assume was the spell and not her. Because if he was looking at her like that, there wouldn't need to be a chastity spell at all. He'd be sleeping alone.

"Mixing godly powers and sex with your mortal lover is a bad idea." He finally conceded after another few seconds of pouting.

"Dionysus!" Hades scolded, putting a hand over his face. "You could have killed her!"

"I thought I had," He admitted soberly, eyes locked onto Ariadne. "She's not taking it as seriously as I'd like."

"After this winter you want have to worry about that." Persephone reassured him, adding to her husband, "I've offered to turn Ariadne into a goddess as a wedding gift. After they exhibit some self control." She added pointedly when Dionysus let out a small whoop of excitement.

Hades raised a finger. "You already put a chastity spell on her. Doesn't that count as cheating?"

Persephone sniffed. "They need all the help they can get."

ARIADNE woke up the next morning to a shouting match. Crawling out of bed, she stopped to have a drink of wine at the bottle thoughtfully left beside the bed. She savored the taste.

It was never something she had told Dionysus, but wine almost universally tasted bitter to her. She now associated the taste and smell with him and found it comforting, despite never quite enjoying the taste.

After drinking a few cups of wine crouched beside the bed, Ariadne finally tuned into what sounded like an argument getting ready to turn into a borderline riot.

"Absolutely not!" Someone vaguely familiar was howling at the top of their lungs.

"I don't give a shit!" Dionysus was yelling back.

Hm. That wasn't a good sign.

Ariadne stood up with a sigh and staggered out of the bedroom and into the hall, still feeling wobbly. No one spoke, silent and tense. Dionysus was barefoot, fists clenched and eyes gleaming and wearing only low slung pants. Ariadne appreciated the view for a minute before taking in the rest of the room.

Opposite him was Persephone, looking beyond irritated. Her hair was fluffed out around her, crown nothing but metal spikes with sharp-edged tips. Hades stood off to the side, watching the show with raised eyebrows. Ariadne realized she was still holding onto her wine cup and handed it to the nearby Hades. He took it with a confused, startled look, but she was already heading to Dionysus.

Ariadne slid an arm across his shoulders, tugging him into a one-armed hug. "I woke up alone. Positively neglected, I tell you." She stuck her lower lip out and widened her eyes comically wide, and looked at a bemused Dionysus through her eyelashes. "Alone. So alone."

He snorted, tension visibly draining out of him. He wrapped his arm around her waist and tucked his fingers into her sleep pants waistband to cup her hip. "I'm sorry." He leaned over to kiss the tip of her nose. "Forgive me?" He asked with a raised eyebrow and half smile.

Ariadne sighed dramatically. "I suppose I must. Fine. The wedding is back on."

He paled. "What? When was it off?"

"Presumably when she woke up alone." Persephone filled in, hair losing its frizzy puff to coil neatly around her head. "Make it up to her and leave the management of my kingdom to my husband and I."

"What did I miss?" Ariadne looked between them, rubbing Dionysus's arm when he tensed up. Persephone shook her head and left, taking her husband with her and leaving Dionysus to fill in Ariadne.

"That demigod Theseus is here. As a guest." He practically hissed, pupils going thin and sharp in contrasting with his black eyeliner.

Ariadne didn't enjoy hearing that, but didn't care too much about it, either. "Quit letting him live in your head. Do what I did and forget him."

Dionysus blinked. "How did you manage that, after what he did to you?"

Ariadne leered playfully at him, hand sliding from his shoulder down his back to grab a handful of ass. "I focused on the better things I had going forward." He gave her a slow smile, skin darkening on the back of his neck.

She let go of him and stepped back. "But if you want to spend time with him and not me, well." She crossed her arms and sniffed pointedly.

Dionysus rolled his eyes, but didn't stop smiling. "Alright, fine, I get the point." He reached out and pulled her close, pressing a kiss to the crown of her head. "What do you think about mandatory flower crowns at the wedding?"

"I raise you mandatory flower crowns we pick out for the guests." Ariadne agreed, trying not to focus on the delightful shudders the butterflies in her stomach gave her at the thought of marrying her best friend. That beautiful, sweet god smiling at her loved her and wanted to live with her. Forever.

There was the sound of a bull roaring in the distance, so muffled it couldn't have been heard unless it was listened for. A familiar sound, one Ariadne had thought she would never have to hear again.

"Do you hear that?" Her voice was hushed, the tingle of fear creeping up her spine. The feeling of being hunted from afar crept up on her, the sensation pacing of feet approaching with hungry intent.

"I don't hear anything." Dionysus admitted after a minute.

Ariadne waited a moment, but heard the sound again. She swallowed. "We need to talk to Persephone."

They found her around the corner, pressing Hades into a wall and hands fisted in the front of his clothes. "Was that what you heard?" Dionysus teased, but sobered at her expression.

The couple broke apart. "Can you hear that?" Ariadne didn't wait for the other couple to ask what she wanted.

Hades frowned, head tilting to the side as the sound echoed again. "It's...that shouldn't be possible. The Minotaur escaped his confinement." He shared a look with his wife before vanishing, presumably to take care of the escaped soul.

Persephone studied Ariadne with only a thin veneer of humanity, covering up her godly form. "I believe I need to take a trip to talk to the Fates. There is something strange going on. You'll be accompanying me."

Before Dionysus could do more than open his mouth in protest, Persephone had Ariadne by the arm and they were gone.

<hr>

ARIADNE blinked, the world warping around her and Persephone until they were at the mouth of a cave. The carved entrance had beautiful images of weaving and painted with bold colors to bring them to life. There was a curtain of beads over the entrance that seemed to be made of spider silk and millions of tiny drops of mist. It gave the shimmering appearance of a sheet of water, rippling with rainbow refractions.

Persephone let go of her arm, parted the curtain of water and light and gestured Ariadne to go inside. Ariadne looked behind her. It was a cliff with a sheer drop that made the trees at the bottom little more than green smudges. She lurched forward, nearly losing her balance, looking down at the dizzying distance.

Petrified, she threw herself at the cave entrance instead of the cliff edge. Staggering inside the cave, she stopped beside the waiting Persephone. From the inside, it no longer looked like a cave. It looked like the inside of a wealthy woman's house. It was the home of a woman, three of them, in fact. Three scorchingly attractive women that Ariadne had not been prepared for, any more than she had been the potential drop from the cliff.

They stood in a row in front of their guests, hands clasped demurely in front of them, faces empty of expression. "Welcome." The goddesses of Fate chorused together.

"Nnngh." Ariadne said intelligently, flustered. Persephone shot her a knowing look before addressing the other women.

"As usual, I'm sure you know more about why I am here than I do." Persephone said with resignation and no little bemusement.

The three women smiled as one, and Ariadne felt her brain restart when they showcased far too many teeth. Ariadne had thought Demeter had a problem. Demeter had actually been around humans at some point in her life. The Fates... chose teeth that made Ariadne question if they had ever seen a human. Humans did not have teeth like that. Things that lived on the bottom of the ocean had teeth like that.

"We do." The middle one spoke, sounding perfectly normal and not at all with a speech impediment from strange dental choices.

"You wish to know how one of your realm can break free from your control, which should be absolute with the entrance of Princess Ariadne into your kingdom."

Ariadne, hearing it put like that, abruptly also wanted answers. But not about the teeth. She could die or live forever and be happy never knowing that.

The middle one, apparently the spokeswoman, approached Ariadne. "You were born too soon. You were supposed to be born after the Minotaur."

"That didn't happen." Ariadne leaned back as the goddess of Fate leaned forward to peer at her.

"He could not absorb you. You had developed too far by the time he was conceived." She told Ariadne, still studying her front like Ariadne was an interesting woven tapestry with intricate details.

"Is that why I have always pissed him off? Failure to eat me in the womb?" Ariadne grimaced and shuffled half a step behind Persephone. Let her get eyeballed by the strange goddesses.

"Indeed." The Fate told Ariadne. "But he will not eat you now. Not while your fate's thread is tied to his. It is what allows him to defy the rulers of this realm, along with your presence."

"Say what?" Ariadne and Persephone said at the same time.

The middle Fate stepped back to stand with her sisters that were still placidly watching. The one on the far right smiled at them both and answered while Ariadne was repressing her flinch.

"The Minotaur didn't absorb you, that is true. But he managed to tie his fate thread to yours. He used it to find you, always. He is using the connection to your living soul to escape the control of Persephone and Hades in their own realm. A fearsome monster." She seemed impressed, and Ariadne had a feeling the goddess didn't leave her cave too much to deal with the rest of the world.

"How do we sever this connection?" Persephone asked immediately, not wavering when all three sets of eyes shot to and focused on her.

The last Fate stepped forward to stand in front of Ariadne and Persephone. "We sever her thread. With them both dead, you would have complete control again." She made a snipping motion with two fingers. Ariadne felt her breath freeze in her lungs and had half a second to be grateful that Dionysus had not come with them.

# Chapter 18

"IS THERE ANY OTHER way?" Persephone asked, cool as a cucumber at the talk of murder.

The last Fate sighed and put her hands on her hips. "It is the simplest and easiest method."

"No, I'm with her. Any other way?" Ariadne added her input and internally cringed when the Fates turned their heads to her and gave her a slow smile as one.

"Not one we can do." The middle one spoke again. "But you, Princess Ariadne, mistress of the labyrinth, could do it another way." The last Fate walked back to her place in the line of creepy, sexy goddesses.

The three spoke as one, voices echoing and resonant. "There is much we could teach you and much for you to learn."

Ariadne abandoned her dignity and clung to Persephone's robe. "Please." She squeaked, not finishing her sentence of 'please don't let them get me' before the Fates took her.

---

"Thinking about your lover?" The Fate nearest to her clucked her tongue at her slyly. "Don't let your motivation to leave distract you."

Ariadne scowled at the stupid scarf in front of her. They had given her a crocheting hook and a basic lesson on stitches and told her to make a scarf and use the whole ball of yarn if she wanted to leave. It should have been easy. It was easy.

The problem was twofold. First, they kept unravelling the damn thing while she slept. Second, no matter how much she crocheted the scarf before sleeping, it only used half the yarn. Even if the scarf she made was longer than she was tall.

"How does making a scarf teach me anything I need to know?" She jabbed her hook through the weave of yarn, resenting the feeling of being caged once again.

"Nothing, really." The Fate told her, unblinking.

Ariadne shrieked, throwing the whole bundle of thread at the tapestry covered stone wall. "Then what was the point in having me do it!" Respect had gone the way of her sanity and scarf- slowly unravelling and down to a single thread.

Another Fate appeared, catching her nightmare crafting project and unravelling it in front of her, staring her dead in the eye as she did it.. "You know the thread now. The feel of it slipping through your fingers, the pull of it in the weave, how tight it can be drawn."

Ariadne regretted skipping out on her childhood weaving lessons if this was her punishment. "Does this mean I can get on with leaving now?"

The third Fate appeared and grabbed Ariadne's hands and pulled her forward. Ariadne stumbled and was suddenly standing beside the Fate, looking at her unmoving body standing there, eyes closed and arms slack. She could see the weaving threads connecting her to other people, thick and thin and all brightly colored.

The gleaming white rope embedded and curled within her chest like a parasite was rather noticeable and alarming. "I won't ever truly be free of the Minotaur with this tying us together, will I?" She realized, staring in shock.

"We make the thread, weave the thread, and cut the thread." The Fates told her together. "You can do something different."

Ariadne waited. They said nothing. "Do I have to guess, or are you going to tell me?"

The Fates laughed at her, briefly seizing her sexuality and giving her hormones a good shake when they managed to not show their teeth. "You can pull threads free of the weave. We would have destroyed you for this ability before you were conceived for treading on our territory, but-" They do not finish the sentence.

"Finish your sentence, please. I need to avoid being vaporized." Ariadne demanded, not at all polite but very much desperate. She got the impression the Fates were less goddesses and more Primordials shoved into the shells of goddesses. Similar to how the gods assumed the shells of mortals but an exponential, terrifying step up.

The one in the middle tilted her head. "We cannot destroy you, as we cannot destroy each other. We are too similar to unweave from the fabric of the world without risking ourselves as well."

Ariadne abruptly decides she would rather be dead and have Dionysus visit her in the Underworld than fall into the eerie synchronization of the Fates.

The Fate on the left smiled at her. "We sought to give you no reason to compete for our role." Or, Ariadne thought silently, unweaving them from existence. Even the thought felt blasphemous.

The Fate on the right smiled at her. "It wasn't hard. Truly, all we had to do was have you meet the god of wine and madness. It stopped what would have been endless suffering for him and, in time, the rest of the gods. Such as they are now. In turn, you lose interest in manipulating the threads of fate outside the happiness of your immediate chosen family."

"Selfish." The trio agreed. Ariadne isn't sure if they are referencing what is apparently a hoarding power problem on their part or her disinterest in destroying herself to control and 'save' the world. Ariadne decides not to touch that subject at all.

"How am I able to manipulate the weave of fate? I'm just a mortal. Demigod, if I really stretch the definition." She skirted around the more problematic parts of what they had told her.

"For now." The middle one agreed, looking bored. "But once you marry your lover, they will make you into a goddess."

Ariadne tried to stare incredulously at the Fates, but her eyes watered at the strange aura of unreality that was always around them. She rubbed her eyes.

"But that will be later." She hoped. "Right now, I'm not a goddess of anything."

The Fate on the left tsks. "Time is what you make of it."

"We sit outside of it." The Fate on the right clarified, giving her sister an annoyed look. Perhaps not all of them were fond of being vague. "You are not yet conceived and also already dead to us."

The middle Fate finished slyly, "Mortal maiden and married goddess both."

Ariadne did not know what that meant beyond the Fates being creepy as possible. She decided to try to manipulate the connection with her ill-fated twin. Who was she to question the eerie judgement of the Fates? Even Zeus, the king of the gods himself, respected them.

Ariadne studied the thread embedded in her chest. She touched the white rope, feeling its smooth, satiny surface. She gave an experimental tug and felt it slide smoothly both in her hands and eerily in her chest. "If I remove this, there is going to be an enormous hole left. That does not seem like a good thing to have."

"Holes tend to be filled." A Fate agreed, appearing abruptly behind her. With a long elegant finger, she pointed to the next largest thread, red and tangled in a knot around her heart like a protective barrier against the overwhelming presence of the white thread. "That would take its place. Your lover would be pleased. You would never be separated, not for long." The Fate said directly into her ear.

"Given the knot I already have, isn't that already the case?" Ariadne interrupted the creepy, manipulative talk with common sense.

A different Fate cackled. "Too like us indeed. Yes, you both have tied yourselves together quite well already."

Well. It was a good thing he wanted to marry her, Ariadne supposed. Being immortal would solve a lot of potential problems if they were this tightly woven together. Still. It made her wonder if this was what they really meant when speaking of 'tying the knot'.

"How can I have this ability at all?" She asked, bracing herself and gently pulling the white thread free, shuddering at the phantom sensation of her flesh caving in around the hole. "I barely have a fourth of Titan's blood, and none of it related to anything like this. I would be less surprised if they made me a goddess of stars or something."

"Gods don't have to be human to be powerful." A Fate told her idly, watching over her shoulder as Ariadne dragged the thread out.

Ariadne swallowed hard, chills racing down her spine. "The bull my mother slept with was a god?" She wasn't sure if that made the union any less icky or not. She was thinking not.

"The earth gives rise to many kinds of gods, as she always has." The Fate gave an answer that wasn't really an answer with a smirk, then following it up with, "With the power in the blood, circumstance decided the shape of it. Nurture, if you like."

Circumstances like desperately wanting to change her fate as soon as she was old enough to understand what it was and what it entailed. That being a dutiful daughter to her parents meant being complicit in the murder of other people, of innocents.

Her lips thinned and Ariadne resumed working on her project, not sure when she stopped. She finally finished detangling the thread connecting her to her twin, the Minotaur, and pulled it free. A phantom ache bloomed in the empty hollow in her chest, throbbing in time with her heart.

She stared at the limp, now much more threadlike string in her hand. "What do I do with it?"

# Chapter 19

"PUT IT IN THE WEAVING basket." They tell her together from where they have been standing behind her in a creepy row again. Ariadne wanted to burn it into ash and ember, but she put the thread into the basket thrust at her. She wanted to leave eventually, after all. She reviewed her body and sighed at the sight of the thread over her heart, full of knots like clots.

"If I unknot this, will it make the thread stronger or weaken the connection?" Ariadne decided not to turn around and see if they were still watching her. They had smiled when she put the Minotaur's thread in the basket. She didn't want to know why or have to see it anymore.

"Will it make a difference to you?" One of them asked, drifting forward to study her face, once again ignoring personal space like it didn't exist.

"Yes. I love Dionysus and I worked hard to hold on to him. If it means weakening the connection, then the knots are just going to hurt." She told the Fate, angry at first and then sad by the end of the second sentence. Whatever the Fates were, she wasn't sure they knew what love felt like and that probably explained more about the state of the world than it didn't, come to think of it.

"Then it would grow stronger." The Fate told her. "Your desires will make it so."

Ariadne paused, fingernails tugging at the outside of a gnarly knot as a new terror took root. "If we had a fight, and I was really upset at him, it wouldn't weaken or come out, would it?"

"No. Your ability to do this is because you are in our place of power only. Outside here, you will only be able to sense these things and workings will cost you greatly in time and energy." The Fate told her. "Stop delaying and tie yourself to your lover so we may have our home free of guests for a while."

Ariadne snorted. "If you didn't stop time when you had one, it wouldn't seem so long." She pulled the knot gently, untangling it slowly, the thread widening as it came free.

She lost time, tugging gently and petting the string free of knots and watching it for any new knots, knowing intuitively she was pulling them free in Dionysus as she worked on herself.

As the threads came free, she willed them into a weave around her heart like a protective shield and a comforting blanket. Whimsically, she patterned it with ivy that he occasionally wore in his hair instead of grape vines. Gently, slowly, she worked until she was exhausted, eyes burning and hands trembling.

She decided she had done everything she could and stepped back to examine her work with blurry eyes. "Perfectionist." A Fate told her before shoving her, and Ariadne was falling toward her waiting body.

⸻ ◉ ⸻

ARIADNE jerked awake, finding herself being held by a terrified looking Dionysus. "I need so much wine." She groaned, blinking up at him, too tired to lift her head.

"Ariadne!" He choked out. "You're awake."

Dionysus held her like she weighed nothing, as if she wasn't his equal in height. He stroked her face with the back of one hand, the yellow ring surrounding his eyes now his dominant eye color. "Are you okay?" He searched her face for any sign of discomfort or pain.

"I-" She stopped and considered the question, taking stock. "I am now." She told him, laying her head back on his chest.

Ariadne eyed his new ivy crown instead of his usual grape leaves and wondered if she was at fault. "You've switched from grapes to ivy." She touched the waxy leaves with the tips of her fingers. "How long was I gone?"

"Only half an hour." Hades assured her from out of sight behind Dionysus's frizzing mane of hair.

"No, I was gone half an hour." Persephone corrected. "I have no idea how long the Fates were holding onto her."

Ariadne snuggled into Dionysus's chest, not wanting to think about the answer to her own question. "I need to never go back there."

Dionysus held her tighter. "That won't be a problem." He told her. His hand trembled as he picked up a long strip of glittering silver hair. "You've gone completely silver."

Ariadne looked up at the god holding her and smiled at him. He smiled back, worry softening the feral look to his yellow eyes. "I love you. You always have the right number of teeth. Always. Sometimes they get a little pointy, but that's sexy." She sighed dreamily.

Instead of taking the compliment, he turned to the other gods with an alarmed expression.

Persephone put a gentle hand on Ariadne's arm. "We need to know what happened." Ariadne gave the Queen of the Underworld a blank look, mind tuning the words out. Persephone sighed and tried again. "You're almost dead from energy loss. We need to know if the Fates were angry at you for some reason or have taken to eating guests. It's important." She added pointedly to the glaring Dionysus.

Ariadne blinked, the action taking longer than it should have. "Ah." She blinked again, the movement strangely heavy. "They did something strange with time. Something about the future, past and present all being the same." She struggled to focus, exhausted and beginning the shake from it. "It's like they exist outside of time." She murmured, distracted by the thought.

Dionysus leaned down and kissed her, sending a flush of warmth through her. He pulled back, and she inhaled, suddenly without the need to fight off sleep.

"Dionysus!" Persephone scolded, but Ariadne's lover was unrepentant.

"What's mine is hers." He shrugged, tightening his grip on her.

Hades dismissed them both, intent on answers. "Is the warping of time how you lost energy?"

"I don't know." She admitted. "It might have been from weaving the threads of fate."

There was a dead silence as everyone in the realm of the dead stared at her in horror.

"Just mine." She added hastily, then reluctantly, "Mostly. They wouldn't leave until I learned how."

Persephone nodded slowly. "You'll be a goddess of fate in the future. They taught you how to use your powers." Personally, Ariadne thought they just wanted her to not come back or interfere with the games they played.

"The Minotaur was using was using our connection to escape his confinement."

"The rules of the dead don't apply to the living." Dionysus said quietly. "But your fate is no longer tied to him?" He asked carefully, face full of wonder.

Ariadne rubbed her chest. "Not anymore."

"Good." He put his face next to hers and rubbed his cheek against hers. "Mine." He told her in an undertone, making her squeak.

Persephone groaned. "I should have known I could be inviting you two to be all lovey-dovey when I asked you to visit."

Hades slid an arm around his wife's waist. "Ah, but they already met your terms, didn't they?"

Dionysus stiffened and stopped his nibbling of Ariadne's ear to look at the Queen of the Underworld and turn on his puppy dog eyes.

"Fine." Persephone threw her hands in the air. "Fine, far be it for me to argue with the Fates themselves. I'll send the ambrosia to your room." She flipped a hand at them, the other pinching her nose and half hiding her smile.

The sensation of thick water slid over and off Ariadne, making her gasp and Dionysus leer. "Thank you." He broke away long enough to thank the rulers of the Underworld sincerely, before turning on his heel and bolting to their shared room. Ariadne clung to him, laughing into the warmth of his neck.

When they made it to their room, the cup of ambrosia was already on the nightstand. Dionysus set her down on the bed and picked up her hand. "I thought about it, I did. If you don't want to go back, we can live in the mortal realm. Full time." He kissed her palm.

"And if I want, we can live on Olympus full time?" She clarified, watching his expression closely.

"Either way." He said simply.

"Your family is in on Olympus." Ariadne pointed out neutrally.

"They can visit." Dionysus assured her. "Or not." He shrugged, setting her hand back into her lap and leaning back to await her decision. He reached over one handed and handed her the cup of ambrosia. "Thinking is thirsty work. Have a drink while you decide."

Ariadne chugged the drink and tossed the cup to the side. Dionysus stared at her, mouth hanging open. She smirked at him and walked her fingers up his arm. "Probably Olympus. The mortal realm wouldn't be nearly so understanding of all the screaming."

"Am I going to be doing a lot of that, then?" Dionysus asked breathlessly. As her hand reached his neck, he arched it into her touch.

Ariadne looked him in the eye and then pushed him flat against the mattress. "Yes."

Did you love *No Mortals Allowed*? Then you should read *The Two Lives of Ariadne*[1] by Honey Beezleigh!

[2]

Dying wasn't part of the plan.

Ariadne's plan was: help her husband, Dionysus get recognized as a god by his father and accepted on Olympus. Her husband elevates her with him, making her a goddess. Simple.

But then she dies. Critically, before her husband is recognized as a god.

It turns out the dead are terrible gossips, and the rumors coming in about her husband are starting to get ugly...

Read more at https://honeybeezleigh.com/.

---

1. https://books2read.com/u/m2EQjR

2. https://books2read.com/u/m2EQjR

# Also by Honey Beezleigh

**What If Myth**
No Mortals Allowed
The Two Lives of Ariadne
The Wrong Princess

Watch for more at https://honeybeezleigh.com/.

# About the Author

Honey Beezleigh loves to read, collect blank journals to fill in "someday", feed her feline overlord and drink too much tea.

Read more at https://honeybeezleigh.com/.